NINE DAYS A QUEEN

NINE DAYS A QUEEN

THE SHORT LIFE AND REIGN
——— *of* ———
LADY JANE GREY

ANN RINALDI

HARPERCOLLINS*PUBLISHERS*

Nine Days a Queen:

The Short Life and Reign of Lady Jane Grey

Copyright © 2005 by Ann Rinaldi

of America. For information address HarperCollins
Children's Books, a division of HarperCollins Publishers,
1350 Avenue of the Americas, New York, NY 10019.
www.harperchildrens.com

Library of Congress Cataloging-in-Publication Data
Rinaldi, Ann.
Nine days a queen : the short life and reign of Lady Jane
Grey / Ann Rinaldi.— 1st ed.
    p.   cm.
Summary: Lady Jane Grey, who at fifteen was Queen of
England for nine days before being executed, recounts her
life story from the age of nine.
ISBN 0-06-054923-8 — ISBN 0-06-054924-6 (lib. bdg.)
1. Grey, Jane, Lady, 1537–1554—Juvenile fiction. [1. Grey,
Jane, Lady, 1537–1554—Fiction. 2. Kings, queens, rulers,
etc.—Fiction. 3. Executions and executioners—Fiction.
4. Great Britain—History—Henry VIII, 1509–1547—
Fiction. 5. Great Britain—History—Edward VI,
1547–1553—Fiction.] I. Title.
PZ7.R459Ni 2005   2004006490
[Fic]—dc22   CIP
                                                  AC

Typography by Amy Ryan
1 2 3 4 5 6 7 8 9 10
❖
First Edition

To my dear friends
Marilyn and John

I don't know what they are going to tell you about me. But be careful what you believe. That was the crux of my sixteen short years on earth and a matter of everyday concern—that I always be careful of what I believed. And whom I believed.

Your life can depend upon it.

This much is true. I was born in the fall of 1537, within a day or so of Edward VI, son of King Henry VIII by Jane Seymour. I was named after her.

I was the great-granddaughter of Henry VII. I was cousin to Edward VI, and it was always thought I should marry him. Three years after I was born, my sister Catherine was born, and five years after that my other sister, Mary.

It is not true that I was a prissy little scholar. Yes, I loved to read and even study, but I liked my fun, too. Because of what happened to me, they never speak of me in terms of having had fun, but I did. When at court, I enjoyed a game of quoits. I enjoyed playing with my dog, teasing my sisters, and attending masques and parties.

I had plenty of opportunity, too. My parents were the Duke and Duchess of Suffolk. As if that isn't of enough eminence, my father, Henry, was the third Marquess of Dorset. I grew up at Bradgate, my father's hunting palace. It had some two hundred servants. Outside was a tiltyard, where my father practiced at jousting; an enormous gate-house; and two magnificent towers. It was surrounded by six miles of park, beyond which were the slate quarries my family owned, and a lake, and beyond that the forest of Chartley.

The servants' cottages huddled somewhere in between it all. But our manor was surrounded by formal gardens and brooks, ferns, rocks, ancient oaks that loomed against the rose-colored brick walls of the guard house. Bradgate was five miles from the city of Leicester. It was built in the old style of castles, for defense. The receiving room was large enough to hold a dozen knights in their bulky armor.

You would think I could have been happy.

It was an idyllic place for children. But it was as if the gods, or my mother, deemed that I should rarely be happy. Therefore I was always miserable at home.

I don't know what made my mother so harsh. Mayhap that Mary was born a hunchbacked dwarf. Maybe that Catherine was more beautiful than I, and she only a second daughter. Maybe my mother had just too much royal blood in her. Enough of it can drive you mad. But she managed to enjoy life always, and yet make all of us miserable all the time, but most especially me.

Her scoldings were constant. I never did the right thing, no matter how hard I tried. She ranted and raved at me, calling me names, slapping me and pinching me and beating me.

Mayhap it was that I was fifth in line for the throne. For I came after Edward and his half sisters, Elizabeth and Mary, and then my own mother, who, because she was not young enough to bear an heir, would waive her right for me.

But she would torment me first, making me pay for a privilege I never wanted and never dreamed I would ever have.

My mother was the elder daughter of Charles Brandon, Duke of Suffolk, and Mary Tudor, the sister of Henry VIII. Everybody knows Henry VIII was a roaring maniac of a man, demanding what was his and even what wasn't. Cruel and vengeful and lustful and always angry. Six wives it took to becalm him, and when he died, he still went a-roaring to that appointment while on his deathbed. So why should my mother be any different? I do not hope to explain her.

What chance did I have to earn her love?

Love did not figure in the fabric of our days.

I was treated like a boy. Certainly I was educated like one, which didn't displease me in the least—if they had only left me to my Hebrew and Greek and Latin studies, my playing of the virginals, my games of shuttlecock. But no, mother was always there, chiding me to go out riding, hunting, racing off in the forest to drag back some venison. I didn't care for it. I wanted to be left to my books. She called me a prissy boots. She called me a white-faced chicken. She called me worse.

Still, somehow I grew to the age of nine years. In a house full of servants, never alone, I yearned for silence. I was groomed by my parents to be queen regent at the very least someday, if I wed Edward VI. I watched my parents' predatory ways as they pursued successful men and well-attached women, fashion, material wealth, and power.

If someone had any of the above, I was to bow and scrape to them. If I didn't, I was punished. Position was all. How they entertained! They had masques and entertainments and cockfights. How they gambled! How they played and rode and hunted and danced. How they traveled, from castle to castle, with a hundred yeomen of the guard at the ready, secretaries, dressmakers, ladies-in-waiting, servants, and footmen.

It was my life, all I knew for nine years. And what right had I to complain? One stayed close to one's parents. One didn't think for oneself. Outside in the world, they were burning heretics at the stake, beheading those accused of treason, which could be anything, depending on the mood of the King.

It was my life until the day we were walking in the gallery of one of my father's other country homes that had once been a monastery, taken from the monks when Henry VIII broke with Rome. They said monks killed in the taking haunted it.

My father and I saw the skeleton arm holding the bloody axe. My mother didn't see it. My mother never saw any omen that was staring her right in the face, if it interfered with her pursuit of pleasure. And right after that a message came from the King.

⌒ TWO ⌒

The messenger brought a letter from the King and a small purse filled with gold sovereigns. He was young and yellow of hair, and dressed in the green-and-white livery of the King. His horse's trappings were of the same colors. Likely he was the son of a nobleman and would be Lord This or Sir That someday. He was handsome, and I smiled at him and sent one servant for a bucket of water for his horse and another servant for a mug of ale, which the messenger, whose name was Robert, drank greedily. He spilled some on his chin, and I gave him my pocket square to wipe it, and he said thank you and stuffed the square inside his doublet.

The late-afternoon sun filtered through the giant oaks' branches and cast shafts of light like poured honey onto the green, where peacocks strutted and we stood. I patted his horse's head while it drank from the leather bucket.

One is never too young to make eyes at a boy, especially if he is of noble birth. My nurse, Mrs. Ellen, told me that. Still, all I could think was, *What if mother ever caught me making eyes at Robert!* But then I was so carefully watched, I seldom had the chance to make eyes at any young man.

My parents came out the great front door then and gave the reply to Robert, who bowed and promised to deliver it with all haste.

I watched him ride off. He was graceful and very beautiful on the horse. It wasn't until he'd ridden off that my parents told me what was in the message.

"You're to go and pack," my mother said, "and Mrs. Tilney will accompany you."

Mrs. Tilney was my gentlewoman. Before I had a tutor, she had taught me my letters and sums, taught me how to curtsey, how to behave at table, everything.

"Where?" I asked.

At first I thought it would be a visit to Princess Mary, that she was ill. She was always ill with one thing or another. Oh, we got along well enough, although she was near thirty by now, but she was a maddening Catholic. Drove you to distraction with her Catholic ways. She was the daughter of Catherine of Aragon, the King's first wife, and was estranged from her father because of her religion.

There was a great fight in England in those days,

between the Catholics and the New Religion. King Henry was Catholic, though he had broken with Rome and declared himself the head of the church.

Or was I to visit Princess Elizabeth? Is that what was in the message?

She was the daughter of the King's second wife, the impertinent and beautiful Anne Boleyn.

King Henry put Princess Mary's mother aside to wed Anne Boleyn. This did not make for good relations between Mary and Elizabeth. Eventually he had Anne's head cut off.

His third wife was Jane Seymour; his fourth, Anne of Cleves; and his fifth, Catherine Howard, whose head he had cut off too.

Now he had Katharine Parr. I'd never met her.

Very well, I'd visit Elizabeth. I liked Elizabeth, who was thirteen to my nine, beautiful as her flaming red hair and no less brazen.

Then they told me whom I was going to visit. None other than Katharine Parr, the King's sixth wife. She had requested my presence in her court. And that of Mary and Elizabeth. And even Edward.

"She wants to bring the King's family back together," my mother told me.

Well, she was a brave lady, Katharine. But then, she was brave enough to wed the King in the first place, wasn't she? Rumor had it that she loved Thomas Seymour, Lord High

Admiral. He and his brother, Edward Seymour, Prince Edward's uncles, were now friends with my parents.

"I don't want to go," I said. "Why must I?"

That's when my mother grabbed my arm and shook me viciously. "Are you mad? Not go to court when you are invited? After everything we've done for you?"

My sisters had come out of the house then to watch. A scene always broke the boredom of the day. "I'll go," Catherine said. "Why can't I go?"

Of course she would. She'd prance right into the King's presence chamber and entrance him, beguile him with her flowing yellow hair that the breeze lifted from her shoulders just then. But she hadn't seen the bloody axe that very afternoon, had she?

"Don't you want to see Edward?" Mary asked.

Dear little Mary with her sparkling eyes. She knew how I felt about our cousin Edward, because I'd confided in her after visiting him at Havering Bower, where he was cared for by Lady Margaret Bryan. I did want to see Edward. He was betimes my only friend in the world.

"Court is dangerous," I told my mother.

"Life is dangerous. Besides, you are trained for it." She slapped me. "Everything we've educated you for leads to this moment."

"Go and get ready," my father said. He didn't slap. I loved him for it. But it took me longer than was sensible to understand that the reason he didn't was because she did.

And that he was more to blame for letting her.

"Can I have the purse of gold?" I asked.

I knew better. They'd put it to their own use, and I'd never see it again. I went. But not before sticking my tongue out at Catherine.

⌒ THREE ⌒

I had been trained for court, trained to curtsey, to kneel before the King, to play the virginals and lute with my eyes lowered, to keep my mouth shut and my ears and eyes open and learn what was going on this day with the King. To dance, to simper, to laugh at all the King's jokes and be modest and compliant. Not to act as a spy for anyone who wasn't in favor with the King. Not to look at the bandaged sore on his leg.

It never closed, and they said that Katharine Parr was the only one who knew how to attend to it properly. Once it did close, and they said the King's face went black for twelve days. And he near died.

But one does not speak of the death of the King, for to do so is treason.

How one is to remain modest when escorted in travel by sixty men at arms, two maids, and a nurse, I do not know. Traveling as such was an embarrassment to me. I would, if I had my way, go dressed as a boy, with the white and green colors of the King, on my own horse. I would ride up to Westminster Palace, dismount, hand the reins to a servant, smile at the dogs that would crowd around me in the courtyard, stride past the men at arms, and go into a back entrance, to the kitchen, and have some ale and meat and bread with the servants, and there really learn what was going on with the King. But my life was not of my own choosing.

Edward, Elizabeth, and Mary were already at the palace before me. We hugged and kissed, even Mary, who could drop her frozen face on occasion and stop acting as if she had just come out of a nunnery, and smile and laugh. We were led to our apartments and traveled back and forth, visiting. Mine were draped in green, tapestries and bed hangings. My bedchamber had carved oak furniture, three chests, a large stone fireplace, a stained-glass window, and a darling turret.

Carved wooden dolls sat on the window seat, amongst embroidered pillows.

"Katharine did all of this," Edward said. "She's trying to make us feel at home."

We were given spaniel dogs to play with and they

romped back and forth between the apartments. Edward did not look good, but then, he never looked good.

"My cough is better," he said. "Lady Bryan sent for an apothecary, who gave me new medicine."

But there were dark circles under his eyes. How different from Elizabeth, who was bursting with health.

Edward was the only one who'd met Katharine Parr. "She is a most gracious lady," he told us as we gathered in his apartments. "She wants to bring us all together with the King. I haven't seen him in months."

"She gave me some new dresses," Elizabeth said.

I looked at her. I envied her green silk, which set off her hair. My gray silk was as dull and drab as I felt my hair was compared to hers. "Have you been restored to your proper rank, cousin?" I asked. "Am I now to call you and Mary 'Princess'?"

"Not yet." Mary sighed deeply. "But even if we were, you are to call us by our names. Isn't that right, Elizabeth?"

Both had been declared illegitimate by their father in one of his fits of anger and were to be called "Lady," and not "Princess."

We were brought mild mulled wine and sweetmeats by servants. We sat around and caught up on events in each of our lives. It felt so good knowing I was wanted here and favored and did not have to be afraid of my mother storming in to scold me for some minor offense.

"Are you still good at playing hoodman blind?" I asked Edward.

He smiled and said he was.

Mary looked older than the last time I had seen her. She looked over thirty, and that was not good for an unmarried woman.

"What else does anybody know about Katharine Parr?" Elizabeth asked.

"She's sweet," Edward said. "And innocent. Too innocent. But she is good to my father. And he so much needs someone to be good to him now. His leg is getting worse."

"She was once wed to Lord Borough, old and wealthy," Mary told us, "then to Lord Latimer, also old. They lived in Yorkshire. She was in love with Thomas Seymour, the Lord High Admiral and one of your uncles, Edward. But that was before the King spoke for her."

"She is brave," Elizabeth put in.

"She has a good head on her shoulders," Edward said, and just as he said it, he minded what he had spoken, and we all looked at one another in horror.

"May it stay there," Mary whispered as if in prayer. And she crossed herself.

Elizabeth said nothing, but I saw her pale. Her mother had been beheaded when she was just three. She never spoke of it. But I wondered what she felt and how she could live knowing about it.

Just then bowls of water for washing were left by servants. Clothes were laid out, and we were sent to our individual apartments to dress for supper and meet the King's sixth wife.

"Have they betrothed you yet?" Edward asked when we were alone.

"No."

"Would that we could wed, dear Jane." And he smiled at me.

I looked into his deep brown eyes. They had flecks of gold. His brown hair was curly and soft. Already his shoulders had started to grow in the way of a man, though he was thin. His intelligence was finely honed. He spoke Italian and French, as well as Greek and Latin.

"But I must wed someone from another realm," he said gravely, "someone rich, because the coffers of England are empty from my father's rash spending and the ruinous wars with France and Scotland."

"Hush," I told him. It was dangerous to talk so.

"We are, neither of us, our own persons. Now, I tell you this as your dear friend. Be careful of Sir Thomas Wriothesley, the King's chief counselor. He looks to make trouble for Katharine."

"Oh no."

"She has the mettle to go up against him, don't worry. Go now and I'll see you at supper."

People often told me I seemed older than my years. If I was, it was because I had to be. We all did, Edward and Elizabeth and myself. We had to be, in order to survive in the world our grown-ups had made. There was no place in it for children. To protect ourselves we had to be aware of their every facial expression, every gesture, every change of tone in their voices.

The King himself came to usher us into the dining chamber. He was such a large man, dressed in red velvet and white ermine and bejeweled. His girth was great. We all knelt before him, and waited until he came to each of us to raise us up. "Mrs. Cornwallis, my confectioner who makes my puddings, has prepared a special dessert for tonight," he told us. And: "I have a pelican now. He's been sent to us from New Found Land."

"That is America," Edward said.

"Yes," said the King, and he patted his son's head. "I see you are up with your studies."

To me he said: "Your grandfather was a gentleman of the Privy Council, and a good man. We hear good things about you, too."

"Thank you, my liege," I answered.

I was pleased. And I took pride in the fact that I knew how to act at table. I knew to throw my napkin over my left shoulder and always to leave something on my plate, for it would be given to the poor who were begging outside the palace gates.

The King took his place next to Katharine at the high table. But he was soon up again, walking around, talking with the Earl of Essex, some ambassadors, a cardinal, and a dark-visaged man in black whom I assumed to be Sir Wriothesley.

The King's face was puffy. He limped. His eyes were almost lost in his plump face. His mouth was small and smiled a lot, but there are those who said that when moved to anger, it was as if God were speaking. People cowed.

Not that night. Before the supper was over, he disappeared with the Earl, and they returned after a while dressed in the fashion of Turkey, bearing scimitars and accompanied by six men dressed as Prussians. There were also torchbearers made up as blackamoors, and they all put on a skit for us.

Naturally the King won in a mock fight and we all applauded. It was not difficult, even in his disguise, to determine which was the King.

"He loves skits and masques," Elizabeth said. Poor Elizabeth. I felt sorry for her. Exuberant as she usually was, she seemed pale and waiflike now in the presence of her father. *She's afraid of him,* I thought, *much as I am of mine.*

I know she yearned for his love. The same as Mary and Edward did.

After the skit the King reappeared wearing a doublet of blue and crimson, slashed with cloth of gold. And there was music and dancing.

I danced with him once! I actually danced with the King. And he was gentle and kind, raising me up from my initial curtsey, speaking kind words to me of my family, his huge bejeweled hands gentle, his voice purring. I felt every inch the worthy lady as he led me through the steps. I felt his presence near overcome me.

~ FOUR ~

Katharine was not pretty but she had a lively, pleasing appearance. This night she wore a rich red gown with a stand-up collar and a jaunty feathered cap.

I went with her to her apartments, which she kept richly furnished with curios and gifts from the King. She also kept greyhounds and parrots. I tried not to stare, but I couldn't help it.

"You made a good impression on the King," she told me. "And on me. He says I may have you stay with me as a maid of honor. Do you wish that?"

Stay with her? I was still afraid and part disdainful of court life. But oh, not to have to go home and endure my family's displeasure with me all the time. "Oh, my lady!" was all I could say.

In her hand she had a dish of morsels from supper for her two greyhounds, who came around sniffing.

"Lady Latimer, Lady Latimer," one of the parrots kept repeating. I went over to them. I loved birds. "My love, my love," the bird said.

Katharine covered their cages so they would go to sleep, and we sat. "So you shall be a maid of honor then. I am told you are schooled in the classics and can speak many languages. How old are you, Jane?"

"Nine."

"Your parents have done a good job."

I made a face.

She smiled. "It is one reason why I ask you to be part of my household. I have heard how they treat you."

"Heard? How come you by such information?"

"There is not much the King does not know about the lives of his people. When he takes action, he does so for a reason. Thus he took action to have you come here. I am pleased with you, Jane. Would you like to see my gowns?"

And she took me into her robing room, where two of her women were stitching. "This is Lady Elizabeth Hoby and Lady Jane Lisle," she said, introducing us. "Ladies," she told them, "this is Lady Jane Grey and she is my new personal companion. I intend that she be closer to me than the greyhounds."

Everyone laughed. Then she showed me the gathering of gowns. "All the silk for them comes from Antwerp," she said. "I shall now show you my weaknesses, Lady Jane Grey."

There were gowns aplenty, in all colors, of all fabrics, bejeweled and plain.

"These over here come from Baynard Castle," she said. "They once belonged to Catherine Howard."

"Ohhh," I said. Then I started to speak. "But," and then I stopped myself.

"Aren't I fearful of wearing gowns from a queen who had her head cut off? No." And she arranged them carefully on the rack. "No, Catherine caused her own demise by living a loose life as a girl. It was bound to come out sooner or later. The King could not condone such actions. Suppose it was bandied about in Scotland or France? His enemies would laugh at him."

Before I had a chance to reply, she was showing me her shoes. Dozens of them, all kinds again, cork-soled, velvet, shoes trimmed with gold. "I have a weakness for shoes, too," she said, "and flowers. The King indulges me."

Then, back in her private chamber I saw a book on a table near her bed. I loved books. "What is that?" I asked.

She picked it up and gave a half smile. "Tyndale's translation of the holy scriptures," she said, "a prohibited book. But I keep up with the New Religion," she told me. "The one started by Martin Luther."

I knew danger when I heard it, and said nothing. Again she said that while the King was yet Catholic, he indulged her, and she gave me a tract explaining some of the New Religion and sent me to bed.

Outside, the hallway was dark now except for torches burning on the walls. Shadows leaped in front of me, and I was glad to see my little spaniel rushing to meet me. "I must name you," I told him as I patted his head. "But what?"

"How about Tyndale?" a voice said. And I drew back, startled. The spaniel growled.

Out of the shadows stepped Sir Wriothesley. Blocking my way, he stood. "A fine name, isn't it?"

"You were listening," I accused.

"Lady Jane Grey, what a lovely plain name for a lovely plain little girl," and he stroked the side of my face with his hand.

"Stand away, sir." I tried to sound brave.

"Oh!" He held up a hand, palm outward and stepped back. "Never would I offend the new little lamb who's been brought to court. I know your father well, lass. Never fear. You have nothing to fear, if you have a vigilant and reverent respect, and eye, for His Majesty. Do you?"

"I shall serve him well," I said.

"Yes, then mayhap you will let me see what you have in your hand?"

It was the Lutheran tract Katharine had given me. "It is my own, sir, not for sharing." He knew what it was, to be sure. Now he would prove I was a troublemaker. I trembled thinking what he would do with that information.

He took it. "You are a believer, then?"

"I was being polite to Katharine."

"Yes. The King indulges her too much. You know that the New Religion is frowned upon by His Majesty, do you not?"

"He still considers himself Catholic, though he believes not in many aspects of the church anymore. He is the head of his own church here in England." I recited that which I'd been taught by my tutor.

He handed the tract back to me. "You can serve His Majesty well by telling me how far Katharine goes with Martin Luther's madness. That is how you can serve your King."

"You mean spy on Katharine?"

The hand came forth again, this time to my chin, and two fingers touched my neck. "Let us say 'protect' Katharine. From herself. I would speak to her about her readings, her beliefs, but it is not my place to do so. If you keep me informed, I can monitor how far this goes. I am sure right now it is just trifling on her part, would you say?"

"I would say, yes," I responded.

"If you keep me informed, a good report will go back to your parents. If not"—and he shrugged beneath the black robe—"well, then, they will be disappointed in you."

So he, too, knew how my parents treated me! That

they would beat me if a bad report went home. I felt a sense of dread. Already the intrigues of the court were being woven around me.

I said nothing. I was trembling. At my feet the spaniel was trembling. I liked this man not, yet I knew I must have continued dealings with him. I must protect Katharine yet not endanger myself. How to do this?

When I again looked up, he was gone.

Disappeared, as if he had never been.

I was shaking so much, I turned and ran back to Katharine's apartments, knocked on the door and was let in by Lady Jane Lisle.

"What is it?" Katharine saw my distress immediately.

Not thinking, I rushed into her arms. And she embraced me. "Dear child, what has frightened you?"

I told her. Wriothesley. "That old fool," she said. "He must have been in here, hiding behind the tapestries."

"But he has the ear of the King," I wailed.

"So do I, dear. Don't let him frighten you. I'm sorry if I got you in trouble."

"Does he have the right to listen in other people's rooms?"

"I have enemies, Jane," she told me. "Wriothesley would catch me in treason. I am loyal to the King in all things, even his religion. I am allowed to read, aren't I?"

"Oh, madam." I hugged her again.

She made as if to take the tract from me, but I held on

workers in his palace. And then, in the cold of the New Year, suddenly things did not go well for him.

In January he lost fourteen captains to the French in a skirmish at Saint-Étienne, France. In February he was laid up with a fever, and Katharine had to nurse him. When he got out of bed, he played at cards. And lost.

In what spare time she had, the Queen was writing a new devotional work, but it was more Protestant than the King liked, so it would not be published.

Sir Wriothesley, who had been lying low, still wanted to convict Katharine of treason. He wanted her out of the way for his own ends.

Lent came early. And Wriothesley came to action. He arrested a famous court preacher for heresy, had the man tortured, and under questioning, the man gave names. Among those names were several courtiers and a woman from Lincolnshire named Anne Askew.

She was a friend of the Queen.

They put her on the rack, but she refused to name names. The King gave permission and she was burned at the stake, though Katharine begged for her life.

The Queen was furious. And frightened. It was an early encounter for me with what lay beneath the beautiful trappings at court, although I had always secretly feared them. And there would be more to come.

⌒⌒

to it fast. "No, I won't let Wriothesley tell me what to read either," I said.

"Hide it well in your rooms, then."

I promised her I would. Then I took my spaniel and went to my apartments to try to sleep. But I could not, and I lay for a long time in my bed, my spaniel next to me. What a comfort he was. He seemed to know that I had troubles, and I fell asleep finally with my hand on his head.

FIVE

Elizabeth, Edward, and Mary went to their homes the next day, but I stayed on.

For a year.

I was to accompany the Queen everywhere, and since she was often in the company of the King, so was I. Unlike the other ladies-in-waiting, I did not make her bed or comb her hair or help her dress. I was to hold her hand when she walked. Admire the flowers in the knot garden with her. Play post-and-pillar, prisoner's base, and shuttle-cock, or bowls, tennis, quoits, or chess on the game table in her room that the King had commissioned for her, and which was inlaid with pearls.

The King was kind to me—kinder than my own father had been—and so I paid little heed to the stories I heard of how he had burned monasteries, imprisoned monks, razed churches if they preached against him, and burned heretics at the stake. Instead I listened to stories about how he had made the court of England a place where intellectuals gathered, where artists, songsters, and poets came from all over the world. How he advanced the study of astronomy, and betimes made his own remedies for himself and others who were ill. How he refurbished his father's dull palaces into places of beauty. How his court now rivaled those of France and Italy.

Anyway, I had all I could do to mind my own affairs.

I named my spaniel Pourquoi at the suggestion of Katharine. Christmas came and I helped with the festivities. We oversaw the hanging of holly and evergreen. We even went downstairs to the enormous kitchens to give sketches of the sugared confections we wanted for the feast. The King was fond of festivities and tradition, especially Christmas. On New Year's Day we gave gifts.

Katharine gave the King a clock-salt, which was a clock and a salt shaker combined. It also had an hourglass, two sundials, and a compass. The King loved things that ticked and buzzed and told him the hour. Elizabeth gave Katharine a 117-page translation of some poem from French to English. Of course, Katharine loved that. I gave her the skin of an orange, intact, stuffed inside with vials of her favorite perfume.

The King gave gifts to everyone, even the lowliest of

I was with both the King and Queen the day they argued, not over Anne Askew, but over a fine point of religion. They often had lively discourse between them. The King could not abide anyone who was dull, who could not play verbal tennis with him. But when did you stop and when did you go on? The lesson was to be learned, apparently, by each one on his or her own.

I was embroidering a pillow slip. We were in the privy garden on that fine day in May. Katharine was so busy making her theological point that she forgot the King did not wish to be bested. Ever. And when she left, he sulked.

"Nothing much to my comfort in mine old days to be taught by my wife," he grumbled to Wriothesley.

"Methinks, sire, that she might be harboring views of which thou would not approve," I heard Wriothesley say as I gathered my things and left.

"Examine the books in her closet," I heard the King say. And from the corner of my eye, I saw Wriothesley fair dance out of the privy garden to his task.

I could not tell Katharine. I could not get to her before he got to her apartments.

Still, I like to think that when the time finally came, that fall, I saved Katharine's life.

I was walking in the lower gallery of the palace when one of my ladies found the paper. The King's summer Progress, in which he traveled throughout his kingdom, was over. Outside a fierce rain was falling, more sleet than rain, pelting the windows, making one glad one to be inside where there were cheery fires. I was headed to my room to do some reading.

The paper was apparently hidden just behind a tapestry. My lady found it and brought it to me, and I read it.

It was written by Wriothesley. And it was *a warrant for Katharine's arrest so she could be questioned.* I ran with it to her chambers.

"Katharine, Katharine!" I burst in, not bothering to knock. She was at her beautiful oaken desk, writing. She was laboring over a new devotional work comparing the King to Moses.

"What is it, Jane? You look terrible. Is the King ill?"

"No. I found this. It's . . ." I could not bring myself to say the words, but thrust the paper at her. She read it and held it to her bosom.

"Wriothesley. He hopes to accuse me of treason!" And she moaned and stood, near to fainting, then fell on her bed, crying.

Nothing I nor any of her ladies could do, could stop her. She clutched that terrible paper and cried and moaned and screamed in a very un-Katharine-like manner. "Someone do something," one of her ladies said. "Do something, Jane. You're close to the King. Go and tell him what a state she is in."

I was afraid, but I went. All the way down the hall I

could hear Katharine's screams, as if she were already fed to some wolves. I ran past stained-glass windows against which hail rapped like icy fingers at my heart.

How had this paper come to be? It could only be if the King had allowed it. And if he had allowed it, what would he say to me when I approached him now?

I went straight to his privy chamber, where I knew he was eating alone this day.

Outside stood two men-at-arms. "I must see the King," I told them.

They knew me, of course. I did have some clout, after all. The door was opened and I was announced.

The King looked up from his food, napkin in hand. The table was covered with an embroidered damask cloth and spread with all kinds of fare. Bottles of wine glistened. Silver dishes gleamed and his gentlemen and grooms stood by. I smelled venison, game pies, stuffed oranges. I had never been in the royal apartments before and I hesitated and gasped.

Velvet cloths covered tables, windows, and walls. The windows here were clear, but in front of them hung ornamental birdcages that housed canaries and parrots. The oaken floors shone. And there were clocks all around, carved with roses and pomegranates, a clock that charted how the sea did flow and ebb, one that showed all the days of the year with planets. There were no scented rushes underfoot here, but velvet and woolen rugs.

But it was the huge, snarling steel andirons in the fireplace that caught my eye.

They bore the initials of the King. And Anne Boleyn.

"What is it?" the King asked. "What is that commotion?"

You could hear Katharine screaming from here. I knew that in a moment I would either be scolded and banished from court, never to return again, or embraced. One could never tell with the King. Would he roar and order me out? Order Katharine arrested immediately?

"Sire." I fell on my knees before him. "The commotion is Her Majesty, sire. She is in dire distress."

"Is she ill, then?"

"No, sire, she . . . she . . ."

"Out with it!" Now he did roar and I trembled.

"She has seen the warrant for her arrest. And she is in a private hell, sire, thinking she has so displeased you. No one can quiet her. We fear she has lost her senses."

He was up on his feet. He was so heavy now that he could scarce walk, and the sore leg required him to be helped by his men. "To Katharine's apartments I go," he said. And with a sense of purposefulness I had not seen in him in some time, he strode out of his own apartments into the hall. "Lead, child"—and he raised his hand—"lead the way to your mistress."

I knew what he meant. I ran ahead, telling all I met. "The King approaches. The King would see Katharine." Couriers, ladies-in-waiting, an ambassador or two, and all servants fell to their knees as he brushed past and into her rooms.

I would follow, but I was held back by his men. And soon Katharine's ladies came out also. From inside the door we heard them talking, then heard his soothing words to her, heard her calming down.

"Send for some of my poppy syrup," he bellowed.

It was brought and he gave it to Katharine, and once she was becalmed, he bellowed again: "Send for Wriothesley. Now!" The door opened and I saw him bending over her bed.

Then it closed again. A page ran away. And within ten minutes Sir Wriothesley appeared in the hall with a detachment of guards, thinking he was to arrest Katharine. No one advised him differently. We stepped aside as they went in, then stared through the open door while the King berated Sir Wriothesley with that roaring voice of his.

"Knave! Fool! Beast!" And he beat his chancellor about the head until Wriothesley retreated with all his guards, half running away.

"Now, sweetheart, we are perfect friends again, are we not?" we heard the King say. And the guards closed the door and stood stiffly at attention. And we dispersed.

It was then that I decided that I would never, for all the inlaid pearl tables and closets full of dresses and shoes, be queen.

What good is it to have your initials on a steel andiron in the King's private chamber, if your head has been cut off?

⌒ SIX ⌒

I did not like to ride. Horses frightened me. But it was one of my duties to accompany Katharine, when she and the King rode out. And besides, I had a new green velvet riding habit, made especially for me in accordance with Katharine's wishes, that I felt I should wear.

At home my parents rode all the time. And I stayed inside the house, reading. Here I had to pretend I was happy astride my mount, as we rode through the King's forest and meadows under the brilliant colors and dappled sunlight of that fall morning. We were accompanied by an extended retinue of people, for my parents had come to visit and were chatting away with the King and other members of court, including Edward Seymour and his brother Thomas, uncles of young Prince Edward.

I had a frisky mount, not my usual horse. She had thrown a shoe. Since I was the topic of conversation between my parents and Katharine and the King, I thought I would ride ahead with Sir Thomas and some of the ladies. It was not polite to listen. And above all, my parents demanded that I be polite.

When I tried to rein in my mount, she would not be stopped. She broke away from Sir Thomas, and the ladies screamed at seeing an obvious runaway.

I was terrified and am afraid I screamed also. All I could think of was, *Mother will be ashamed of me because she is such an excellent horsewoman. And now, especially, when Katharine is telling her of all my virtues.*

And I feared for my life, as tree twigs and underbrush slapped against me and seared my face. But then I heard another set of horse's hooves behind me, the snorting of the animal, and Sir Thomas's strong voice. "Hold on, Lady Jane."

So I did, for dear life, while his mount gained next to mine. And then I saw a strong, browned hand reach out to grab my horse's reins and pull her in.

A cloud of dust rose up around us. And there was Sir Thomas Seymour's grinning, handsome face. "Some ride, my lady Jane."

"Oh, my parents will never forgive me."

"I will forgive you." And he laughed. "Anyone's horse can run amok. The trick is to hold on, and you did. You did your parents proud!"

"They won't think so, I'm afraid," I said, near to tears.

He took out a pocket square and gave it to me. He himself wiped my tears. "Your poor little face has more than freckles on it now," he said. "It has welts from the tree branches. Here, don't let them see you cry. When they round that corner behind us, smile and act as if it was all a lark," he advised.

So I did. I even let my mount prance a little. "Bravo, Jane," the King said. And whether he said it to ward off my parents' harsh words or because he meant it, I shall never know. But just then Sir Thomas winked at me and we rode on ahead.

I had seen Sir Thomas often at court, with other courtiers. He was no more than thirty-eight and all the women were daft over him. He had wit, he joked recklessly, he did tricks for the children at court and always had sweetmeats for them. He dressed impeccably, he danced like a true courtier, and he had a voice that sent shivers down the spines of the women. I think he was still in love with Katharine at that time. And she with him. But their eyes never met at court. He never asked her to dance.

He would have been my choice for Katharine, had she not been married to the King.

"Why are you so afraid of your parents?" he asked me now in a low voice.

"Because they'll beat me if I don't meet their expectations."

"Ah. And so you are unhappy at home."

"Yes, my lord."

"In a way, we are all unhappy, Jane." And for the moment this high-spirited man's demeanor became morose.

"Are you, sir?"

"In my own way."

"Is it because Katharine wed the King?"

"Ah, you're a bold little piece. No wonder you get beaten. Yes, it is. But I am young; I can wait, Lady Jane. The King won't live forever."

"Sire!" It was treason even to speak of the death of the King and he knew it better than I.

But he smiled at me. "Would you repeat our conversation, then? I would think the events of a moment or two ago would seal our bond and make us friends."

"We are friends. And I shall not repeat it," I said. But I blushed. He made one blush and he took joy in it.

"I will make you a promise, Lady Jane," he said quietly. "Someday soon I will adopt you. Is that to your liking?"

"Yes, it is to my liking, but how can this be? How will my parents allow it?"

"Adoptions are arranged, even when parents are still alive," he said. "Things can be done. Tell me, do they not wish you to wed Edward, your cousin? Son of the King?"

"Yes, sire."

"Then I will arrange it. I have, shall we say, connections.

And they will turn you over to me. I have been mulling the matter over for some time now, even while I have been watching you at court. You have decorum and manners. I have heard that you read Greek, Latin, and French. You are a precocious scholar. You surpass anyone your age. You should have a good home. I may even sweeten the pot with gold for your father."

He'll like that, I thought.

"Does that please you, Lady Jane?"

I was blushing again. "Yes, sire."

"I promise you," he whispered. "Be patient. Things will come to a good end." And with that he went to join the ladies, so it would not look suspicious, us being so long engaged in conversation.

And that is how I met Sir Thomas Seymour, finally. And that was his promise to me.

That winter my grandfather Brandon lay dying, and I had to go home to Bradgate, where he was being cared for by my mother's people.

He lay on a couch in one of the sunniest chambers in front of the house, looking out on the gray-brown bowling green, at the bare trees, at the hints of frost and the peacocks. I sat beside him where he lay.

Something had overtaken Grandfather Brandon just before Christmas and he became steadily and steadily weaker. He could not sit up. He could scarce take food in his mouth. His voice grew weaker every day.

But he was a handsome man still, with his white beard and his velvet robes. He had been a country gentleman always, ennobled by the present king. He had vast estates in Lincolnshire. He had been in the French campaigns. Been at the coronation of Anne Boleyn. Been a friend as well as servant to the King, and now he lay dying.

My parents stood behind me as Grandfather Brandon weakly grasped my hand. "This child," he said, "is the wisest of all."

And then he lapsed into unconsciousness.

"Smartest of all, indeed," my mother said as she pushed me aside. "You always want the glory, Jane, even at someone's deathbed. Go from this room."

I went. The King had Grandfather Brandon buried in St. George's Chapel, Windsor, at his own expense.

The King's health was failing. I stayed away from him as much as I could because he had frequent explosions of temper. His leg pained him terribly. He spent most of his time in his private chamber anyway, coming out only to walk in his privy gardens.

Only his gentlemen of the chamber and closest servants were allowed in to see him, Katharine, some councillors, and on a special occasion, a foreign ambassador.

He had a special chair made for himself. He called it a "tram" and in it he was carried about to his galleries and chambers. It was made of soft velvet and silk, and it was kept in his secret study with his maps and pictures.

Talk was rife at court about how long he could last. But none dared utter such thoughts in more than a whisper. The royal physicians scurried about telling everyone he was in robust health, and everyone felt sorry for them, for they knew not what to do.

On the seventh of December, he was out taking his exercise. On the tenth, he was laid up with a fever. For Christmas, the court was closed.

Prince Edward wrote his father a letter in Latin, saying he would like to emulate him in virtue, wisdom, and piety.

On January nineteenth even the King's musicians were dismissed. And on Friday, the twenty-eighth of January, he died. It was snowing. Heavily.

I was sent home. Katharine must re-form her household. In the King's will, she was not named Queen Regent as she expected to be, and she was disappointed. She must leave the palace, leave the court.

At home, things were dismal. It was as if someone had stretched a lute string almost to the breaking. People dared not speak, lest Mother lash out at them. It seemed as if everyone was waiting for some word of something.

And then word came, via a messenger, the same young man who had come to fetch me to court so long ago now.

The King's will named me after Edward and Mary and Elizabeth.

Still, I suffered mother's sneers. "You. Fourth in line for Queen. You with the freckles. And you're so short and can't even sit on a horse properly. Never forget, I gave up my claim to the throne for you."

"I don't want it," I said.

So she slapped me. "Don't tell me what you want and what you don't want. I suppose you think you're going to the funeral."

"I know better, Mother. Women are not allowed to attend. But I have been invited to listen to it with Katharine from her closet."

"Oh, so you've been invited. Well then, you'd better get yourself invited back to court by that insipid cousin of yours, the boy king, because you are a nuisance around here."

"I will, Mother. I will."

The heart breaks quietly. No one can hear.

SEVEN

The winter at home was endless that year. And it snowed so much. I played with Pourquoi and he became part of the household, and although I feared the doings of court life, the intrigue, the need to watch my every word and move, yet somehow, at the same time, I missed it. I missed the people I'd met, the music, the masques, the times I had for study, alone.

Here, though our household was smaller, I was never alone. Mother made sure of that. Even when I was doing my studies or when my tutor came, Catherine or Mary was allowed in the room with me. Mother believed that when a young girl was allowed privacy, bad things happened. I don't know what. But the lack of privacy drove me near mad.

And, while I always loved my studies, the schedule was backbreaking. Up at five, prayers at six, then a breakfast of bread, meat, and ale. After that, we visited awhile with our parents, then we studied Greek and Latin until dinnertime. After dinner, it was music, modern languages and classical, or Bible reading until supper. Then we had dancing lessons and needlework before going to bed at nine.

I loved my sisters, and I played with them and told them stories of court, but I knew I would not be going back there to stay. Still, the English had a custom of boarding out children after they reached a certain age. And I sensed that arrangements were being made behind my back.

I waited for Sir Thomas Seymour. The thought of him was like a bright torch in the back of my mind. He had promised he would come for me. Gossip had it that he had wed Katharine in secret, that he was trying to get my cousin Edward, now King, to approve the marriage.

When Edward does that, Sir Thomas will come, I told myself. After all, he did promise. I waited for him like a prisoner in a tower, a princess awaiting her knight who would rescue her.

Finally, one day in March, an exceptionally warm day that promised spring, he did come, with his retinue of people. He rode into our courtyard and dismounted, and he was garbed beautifully, as always. Oh, please let him have come for me, I prayed! Please!

My sisters and I were presented and we curtsied, and then I was asked to play the virginals, which I did with all my heart and soul.

Everyone clapped. There was talk. Of his brother, Edward Seymour, who had become the boy king's Protector. Of the way he kept young King Edward on such a short leash.

I longed to see my cousin Edward. He was now King! How had he taken the honor? I had not seen him since he became King. Would he be able to ward off all the scheming men around him who wanted his power?

Then my sisters and I were sent from the room. From out in the gallery, I listened.

There was an exchange of money between Sir Thomas and my father. I heard my father call him "Admiral," for he had been given the title by King Edward under advice from the Protector.

I heard the words "*alliance*" and "*cousins*."

And then, without seeing me again, Sir Thomas left. I watched through the tall windows of my father's house as he mounted his charger and rode off with his men.

That evening my parents told me I was soon to go to Chelsea Manor to live with Katharine and Sir Thomas. He was now my guardian. I was getting away from here.

The Adonis of the court, with those lively brown eyes, had come for me! I felt joy I could scarce contain, but I did contain it, lest my mother, seeing me too happy, stop the whole business.

My knight had come for me. I was free.

Before I went to Chelsea Manor, I went to see the King.

It was only proper. I had not seen Edward since he was crowned. I found him in his presence chamber. He was not alone, of course. Kings are never alone. His Lord Protector, the brother of my Sir Thomas, was with him.

The presence chamber seemed more austere than when King Henry had occupied it. All the tapestries were gone and only the bare stone walls stood out, with arches in them for candle sconces and other arches for windows. Edward was at a long table covered with a crimson drapery, and Sir Edward stood next to him. Other gentlemen of the chamber stood about.

I knelt before Edward, who was embarrassed at seeing me kneel and raised me up immediately. Then we hugged. "My old playmate," he said. "My cousin. I'm so glad to see you."

"Your Majesty."

"This is my Lord Protector, Edward Seymour."

"I know. I go now to stay with Sir Thomas, his brother, and the Queen Dowager at Chelsea Manor."

"Ah, you are in luck. I wish I could go with you this morning. How are you to go thence?"

"By horse. With guards."

"No, you must take the smaller royal barges down the Thames. Chelsea Manor has its own dock, and it's only three miles outside of London, but what a boat ride! You must, I say. Who is with you?"

"My ladies, Dorothy and Eleanor; my nurse, Mrs. Ellen; and thirty men-at-arms."

"The smaller barges are still all decorated from the coronation two days ago. Did you see me when I was crowned?"

I had. He had looked so small in the vast church, so lost in those red, ermine-trimmed robes, so childlike in the throne in church, it had frightened me. "Yes, I had a good viewing, Your Majesty."

He gripped my hand. "Come and see me often. I command it. I have an idea this is going to be a lonely job. I study with some other boys, but I don't get to see girls that much. Promise me."

I promised. The Lord Protector saw me out. "Give my brother, Sir Thomas, my regards," he said, and I thought I detected a sneer on his face. I knew the brothers did not get along.

Chelsea Manor was a short trip outside of London, even going against the tide on the river. And the small royal barge I rode in was still decorated, with gauze curtains and flowers on its prow. I pretended to be a princess being rowed to meet her knight-lover as we made our way past the scenery on both sides of the river. As we got into the countryside, farmers left their plows to come to the water's edge and wave at us. Country maids threw flowers into the water. *They throw them at the barge,* I told myself, *not me.* But it felt good to be so honored, anyway.

"They're wondering what royal personage is riding here," I told my ladies. And they giggled.

Chelsea was a true manor house, made of rosy red brick, with formal walled-in gardens that sloped down to the river, with sundials, statues and small fishponds, rose arbors and fruit trees. Hollyhocks stood like soldiers. The house was shrouded by giant oaks, and I could see at once that it was one of the modern style, built not for defense, but for enjoyment. Its large windows reflected the late-afternoon light, and I wondered which room would be mine as we approached the small pier.

I was greeted by Katharine, Sir Thomas, Elizabeth, and a whole retinue of dogs. Pourquoi near went mad with excitement. All seemed overjoyed to see us.

"What are you doing here?" I cried to Elizabeth.

"I've been invited to stay, just like you."

"Oh, we'll have a grand time. I wish Edward and Mary were here too."

She laughed. "Edward is now King. Can you imagine?"

"I just came from visiting him. Sir Thomas, your brother sends his regards."

He nodded.

He put an arm around my shoulder. "What's nice about this place is that it's away from the corruptions of court life," he said.

Elizabeth smirked at me, as if to say "Don't believe it." Or did that smirk say something else? It bothered me that I didn't know.

I hugged Katharine, she who had been like a mother to me. I had missed her so, during the long winter months, and told her. "Well, let's hope you never have to leave here," she said, hugging me back.

"As long as Sir Thomas keeps paying your father, you won't have to," Elizabeth whispered.

Elizabeth had changed since I last saw her. She was nearly fifteen but seemed older. She carried herself differently and she had a bosom! I felt like a child next to her. How had this happened? Why did I stay so young in appearance, and how did she come to be so sophisticated?

"Are you adopted too?" I whispered.

"No. One can't adopt a princess."

"Has your title been restored then?"

"Yes. Edward did it. Isn't he a love?"

I nodded yes. "I must ask Sir Thomas if I may visit Edward often."

"Why do you have to ask Sir Thomas?"

"He's my guardian now."

"Oh yes, I heard. You couldn't have picked a more handsome one, I must say."

48

"I didn't pick him, he picked me."

"Oh yes, of course," she said snidely. "After you get settled, come on out and we'll toss around a ball. Unless you're too old for such childish play."

"I too old?" I laughed. "You're the one who's too old, Elizabeth."

She grinned shyly, knowing what I meant.

When we got up to the house, Sir Thomas had the servants take my things inside. "So you're here finally, you little minx," he said. He leaned down to kiss me. I smelled a mixture of horse and musk on him. And his beard tickled. "Yes, sir."

"It won't be all play, you know," he added, suddenly serious. "I've a tutor for you two girls. Elizabeth, why don't you accompany Jane to her apartments?"

We went into the house and Elizabeth showed us around as if she owned the place. "Your chambers are next to mine," she said. Then she whispered, "Get rid of your ladies," so I did, telling them they might have the afternoon to themselves to get settled.

In my apartments, Elizabeth sat back on my bed. "Sir Thomas wanted to marry me before he wed Katharine, you know," she confided.

I stared at her. It could or could not be true. "He's always loved Katharine," I said.

"Yes, but he's mad for power. Why do you think he has you here?"

"I have no power attached to me."

She scowled. "He's promised your father to wed you to Edward someday. They have an understanding between them."

"I know that," I said airily, though I was embarrassed about it now. How serious was it anyway? I'd thought that day on horseback that Sir Thomas had been joking. "He just wants to make Katharine happy, that's why he has me here," I insisted.

She laughed, a trilling sound. "Believe as you wish, but trust no one, that's my motto."

"Elizabeth, you have grown up." I said it half in admiration.

The snide look vanished then. And a sad one came over her. "I've had to. It's the only way to keep from being hurt. And if you'll take my advice, you'll do the same thing, Jane Grey."

Then we went downstairs for supper.

I often thought how lucky I was to be at Chelsea with Sir Thomas and Katharine in the months that followed.

We four made up a family. It felt like a family, and I'd have traded off my own parents in a minute for Sir Thomas and Katharine.

Of course Sir Thomas wasn't always there. As Lord High Admiral—a post bestowed on him by his brother through my cousin Edward, to soothe his feelings—Sir Thomas was away betimes for weeks.

There were, of course, rumors that circled around him like smoke. But then, doesn't every handsome, interesting man attract rumors? I thought heaven itself would have rumors if I ever got there to hear them. These were whispered when company came, of course. And they concerned Sir Thomas having dealings with pirates, taking a share of their bounty, assembling himself an army, being insanely jealous of his brother because he had the ear of the King.

I do know Sir Thomas sent Edward ducats, because the Protector kept him without money. I do know he sent his brother gifts to keep in his good graces.

Needless to say, I worried for Sir Thomas. I knew he was reckless and foolish, and hoped he would not get into trouble with those pirates of his. Whoever they were.

Ah, but when he came home, all worries vanished.

He played with Elizabeth and me at quoits, chess, cards, ball in the gardens, or just plain running and teasing, with our dogs.

The tutor he had employed for us, Mr. Ascham, was patient, yet insistent. Elizabeth and I worked well together with him.

Sir Thomas made me recite for him when he came home, listening with mock severity. He pronounced my Latin and Greek translations superb. But I think Elizabeth, who was brilliant, didn't have to work as hard as I did, and I envied her that. She also seemed to have years of experience behind her that I lacked. One day Sir Thomas told me, "She lost her mother at age three. Her father has mostly ignored her. She's had to exist on her wits alone."

I was near to tears. I could not bear that he took up for her.

Elizabeth and I put on masques for Katharine and Thomas. When company came, we were allowed to stay and visit and were not sent from the room. I adored Sir Thomas. I'd have done anything for him. I thought I'd died and gone to heaven living there.

Then one day in the winter, Katharine told us she was expecting a child.

∽ EIGHT ∽

That winter Sir Thomas was away. But for the most part, Katharine was well. And happy. Never had I seen her so happy. She told us how her first three husbands, both so much older than she, had had children and she'd been a mother to them, but she'd never had children of her own and always wanted them.

I longed to ask Katharine if the rumors were true about Sir Thomas, the pirates, and his raising an army because he was so angry at his brother, the Lord Protector. But I dared not. Could Sir Thomas be so foolish?

Why, even a schoolchild knew that part of the reason the King went on a summer Progress each year, traveling through the countryside, was to make sure none of his subjects had enough private retainers to be construed as a standing army. To have an army was treason. I worried about Sir Thomas.

We spent a lovely, cozy time at Chelsea Manor. Sometimes Katharine, Elizabeth, and I would walk together of an afternoon with our respective ladies. Other times we sat and sewed small garments for the new baby. Sometimes we just sat wrapped in warm cloaks and watched the small boats and swans on the Thames, or played music inside the house. I was never so contented.

I read to Katharine from some of her favorite new religious tracts when she became restless. I made her a sleeping posset with my own hands when she could not sleep. We readied the house with holly and greens for Christmas.

And then the Lord High Admiral came home. And of a sudden everything changed.

One morning I lay abed, wide awake, just listening to the sounds of the house coming alive, when I heard a scream from Elizabeth's chambers. I got up, put on a robe and went to see what was happening.

I stood stock still in the doorway to see Sir Thomas in there in his long nightshirt, his feet bare, leaning over Elizabeth's bed and tickling her. I gasped. In the corner of the room were two of Elizabeth's ladies, but they acted as if they did not know what to do. One had her hand over her mouth. The other had her face half turned away.

"You lazybones, time you were out of bed," Sir Thomas was saying.

"Leave me be, you oaf," Elizabeth shot back.

But Sir Thomas would not leave her be. He continued, lifting a pillow and pretending to strike her with it, tickling her and once even slapping her on the buttocks when she turned over.

I knew I must do something, so I called his name. "Sir Thomas."

He stopped, a pillow midair. "Ah, you want some too, you little minx."

I backed off. "No, sir, I just thought—"

"Nobody asked you to think. You don't when you do your lessons from what I hear from your tutor. Anyway, I'll get to you if you wait long enough."

I ran from the room. Something was wrong with that scene I had just witnessed. It was more than passing strange. It had about it the movements of a ritual, some witchlike thing.

I spent the morning wondering just how much of the witch Elizabeth had in her. According to common gossip, her mother, Anne Boleyn, had been part witch. Her father had ended up fearing her. Hadn't Anne had a sixth finger on one hand that she hid with specially made long sleeves? Hadn't she all but bewitched the King? Hadn't he wanted her burned at the stake, then given in at the last minute and agreed to beheading?

Did Elizabeth, with her sudden womanlike appearance, her rich red hair, have part of the witch in her, too? Had she indeed bewitched Sir Thomas?

I knew right from wrong, certainly, but how could I lay any blame at Sir Thomas's feet? I looked up to him too much. I never mentioned the scene to anyone.

It became a habit.

Every morning Sir Thomas would sneak into Elizabeth's room, ostensibly to wake her.

Every morning came the shrieking from Elizabeth, the pillow fights, the tickling and slapping, the ladies clucking their tongues and rolling their eyes. And Sir Thomas flushed and enjoying himself.

Every morning I made it my business to go inside Elizabeth's chambers and stand there as a witness. Sir Thomas and she both ignored me and continued with their rough playing as if nobody were about. And when he quit, he'd pass by me and tweak my nose. "She's a lazy-bones. You're not. See to it that you don't become one, or you'll suffer the same." And he would walk out of the room.

Always he would throw off Elizabeth's covers before attacking her, to "wake" her. Always she would fight him.

"Why do you allow it?" I asked her one morning.

"Don't be a prude" was all she would say.

"It isn't right, Elizabeth. The two of you like that. Do you know what could happen? You're a princess, second now in line for the throne. You know your brother Edward has a terrible cough and isn't well. Sir Thomas once asked the Lord Protector for your hand, according to your lights, and now this? It could be construed as, as . . ." My voice faltered.

"As what?" She glared at me.

"Nothing," I said.

She laughed. "Flirtation! He's wed. His wife expects a child in the summer."

"Exactly," I said.

"Don't speak to me of it! I won't hear sermons from the likes of you, a short little freckle-faced waif. You make your own flirtation with Sir Thomas."

"I never."

"I see the worshipful eyes you make at him. So does he, don't worry."

I fled the room.

I knew I must do something. The ladies-in-waiting talked if they did nothing else. There were no secrets when it had to do with royal personages. What to do? Whom to go to?

Christmas came and went. I looked to the tradition of it, the customs, the feasting, the company, the dances, the gift giving at New Year's, to erase the terrible knowledge from my mind. All the rest of the day, Elizabeth and Sir Thomas acted with decorum. It was as if I had dreamed this nightmare and it was all mine.

The Thames froze over in January. Afternoons, we sat by the large sunfilled windows and watched the people playing games on its frozen surface. Some children had bones tied to the bottoms of their shoes and were skimming around on the ice. Others pushed stones around with sticks, making a game of it. I was supposed to be embroidering a new shirt for Sir Thomas, when Mrs. Tilney came upon me staring out the window.

"I would speak with you, Jane."

I followed her into my own chambers, knowing this was important. Mrs. Tilney never interfered in my life unless it was important.

Inside the door of my chambers, she turned to confront me. "What are you going to do about this business with Sir Thomas and Elizabeth?"

I set down the shirt I was embroidering for him. "What business?"

"Child, you are there every morning. Or so I've been told. You are a witness to this terrible behavior. Do you know the consequences, if they are found out?"

I shook my head no. Truth be told, I was a bit glad she now spoke of this.

"Why, it's treason. She is now second in line for the throne and he makes bold with her. They could both go to the block if their foolishness is discovered."

A chill ran through me. "What can I do?"

"You must go to Katharine. And tell her. Before it goes any further."

"I? Why must I be the one to tell?" I felt the unfairness of it in my bones.

"Because of your love for Sir Thomas and Katharine. Because you owe them both. Because Katharine trusts you."

"But he'll be angry with me."

She scoffed. "For saving his life? For bringing him to his senses? I doubt it. Now you must do this, Jane. You know you must."

I bowed my head and said yes, I would do it. For I knew, indeed, that I must. But the unfairness of it still stung me, and I knew no good could come of my actions.

NINE

I told Katharine. And she was a true Queen Dowager. She acted like royalty, to be sure. She never betrayed herself, never let a tear fall or a lip tremble.

"Thank you, Jane," she said.

She was abed, though it was full light. I had intercepted the maid and brought Katharine her morning repast. She lay back against the pillows looking lovelier than ever, lovelier than Elizabeth of a morning, and near as young with her flowing hair and her silken gown.

Why was Sir Thomas not in here awakening his wife?

She answered the unspoken question for me. "Men have been known to do all kinds of erratic things when their wives are expecting a child," she told me. "I cannot accuse him of anything. I shall have to wait to see for myself."

If you got out of bed and went to Elizabeth's chambers you would see now, I wanted to say. *For I heard her shrieking as I came this way.* But I kept a still tongue in my head. The whole affair was too onerous for me.

I turned to leave and stopped at the door. "You won't tell him I told?"

"No, of course I won't tell Sir Thomas you gave me this information. He would be most put out with you, though you have done the right thing, Jane, and I thank you."

I did not feel as if I had done the right thing. I felt prissy and proper and a tattletale, and I knew in my bones Sir Thomas would find out it was I. So would Elizabeth. *How can doing the right thing make someone feel so wrong?* I wondered. And then I went to my tutor for my lessons.

The morning sessions went on, but with a strange twist. Now Katharine joined in, going to Elizabeth's bedroom with her husband and making a great to-do out of getting her out of bed.

I stayed away, but I was told of it by a serving maid.

"They do the most odd things. They chase her around the room, and she, princess that she is, just eludes them always, and jumps on the bed, skirts flying."

So then, Katharine was partaking in the early morning romp so as to protect her husband. If there was any gossip outside the house, she could say she was there.

How she must love him, I thought.

I will never wed, I told myself, then knew that was impossible. I was a bargaining chip for my parents, mayhap even for Sir Thomas now that he had taken me under his care. All girls of royal blood were, princess or not. And you were lucky indeed, if you got yourself a patron such as Sir Thomas.

And then, two days later, on a day of February thaw, when the sun seemed a blessing, nothing less, the unthinkable happened.

Katharine caught Sir Thomas and Elizabeth in an embrace in the garden.

I had seen them together there first, merely strolling, although there seemed to be something intimate in their conversation. Sir Thomas had waved at me, and I at him. Then I went into the house, and there was Katharine looking out one of the large windows.

"They are together, then," she said flatly to me.

I could not deny it. I said yes. And she went outside. Oh, I wanted to stop her. There was a death knell in my bones, I wanted to stop her so! But I did not. Why did I not?

I watched Katharine waddle down the steps of the garden. And waddle she did, for she was well advanced in her pregnancy. I turned from the window and picked up a book and tried to read, but to no avail.

I picked up my flute and started to play. My back was

to the door from which Katharine had exited. I was well into my song, practicing, when the door opened and Sir Thomas stormed in.

"Well, I hope you're happy," he said.

I stopped midnote and stared at him. His face was flushed. From the sun I hoped, but I knew better.

"Sir?"

"Don't 'sir' me, Lady Jane Grey. You told her about my morning visits to Elizabeth, didn't you? Making something of innocent play."

I did not answer. He had a violent side. Anger came quickly to him.

"And now you ran into the house to tell her we were in the garden together. Is this how you repay me for my kind-nesses?"

Something in his tone caught at my heart. I put my flute down. "Sir, I never."

Just then Katharine came in, huffing and puffing. Tears were coming down her face. "Thomas, don't blame the girl."

"There is no blame to be put. Nothing happened. Except that she was spying for you." He turned to me. "Is that what you learned at court? To spy? You do it well."

I could not abide this! I ran to him, threw my arms around him, and he held me. I buried my face in his leather doublet. He did not let go, but he said no more.

Katharine spoke. "Thomas, I would speak with you in

our chambers. Leave the child out of it. She is not spying."
She wiped tears from her face and, regally as she could in
her condition, walked from the room.

He followed.

"Please," I said as he walked away from me. I held on to
his hand with both of my own. "Please, Sir Thomas, I did
not send her into the garden. I promise you that."

He pulled his hand away and looked at me sadly. "Trust
is so hard to come by, Jane," he said. "It was one of the rea-
sons I adopted you. You trusted no one. Everybody could
see that. I wanted to give you some sense of, of . . ." His
voice trailed off and he sighed, shook his head, and walked
from the room.

How could he speak of trust, he who had failed Katharine
so? Because he thought of it as innocent play?

Oh, I was so confused. Something was broken in the
house after that. Sir Thomas was too much the nobleman,
too much the knight, too much the protector to mention
it to me again, but I know he never forgave me.

Katharine had caught him in the garden with Elizabeth
in his arms, she told me.

I did not want to think what that meant. I hated
Elizabeth for it, though, for what she had done to us all.
She was truly like her mother, Anne Boleyn.

She was a child one moment, innocent and trusting,

and in the next a witch going after another woman's husband.

And dear Katharine. Who could hurt her?

I caught her crying on several occasions after that, and I wondered how we could all continue to live together in the house. I avoided Elizabeth. It was not difficult to do. She was out and about more than I. Riding, playing at archery, or just walking.

After a week Sir Thomas called me into his study.

"You haven't been speaking to Elizabeth," he said.

I did not deny it.

"That is no way for you to behave. She will be Queen of England someday. You know Edward is not well. And that Mary is always sickly. I would that you speak to her, mend this thing between you. Don't let it fester."

I promised him I would speak to her.

"She is soon to leave us," he said.

I just stared at him.

He was fussing with some papers on his desk. "It is Katharine's wish, and I must honor it. She will be going to Hatfield to stay with a very dependable couple who have stewardship of the place. And I am off at the end of the week for the Isle of Wight. I have ships and men to see to, as well as the country's defenses. I would that you keep Katharine good company while I am gone."

"Yes, sir," I said.

That was all. There was no more joking or teasing between us. He was stern and serious. Then in the next moment I was dismissed.

Elizabeth had a new green velvet archery outfit that fitted her form perfectly. She had soft leather gloves, a perky hat.

"Your outfit becomes you," I said, approaching her as she was taking aim at her target in the fields behind the house. "Green is your color."

"My mother had an outfit like this made. I had to have one too."

I watched as she let the arrow fly and saw it land near the center of the target. "You play well. I could never even hold that thing."

She tossed her head. "Innocent play keeps us all sane, Jane."

What was I expected to say? I minded that someday she would be Queen and I would be obliged to kneel to her. No sense offending her now. Queens had long memories.

"You don't play enough," she chided.

"I would rather read."

"But you chide others who do."

"I chide no one," I said. "Shall we correspond when you are at Hatfield?"

"Yes. I would like that. You must let me know the instant

Katharine's baby is born. It is to be a boy, you know."

"How so?"

"Sir Thomas has been seeing astrologers and fortune-tellers. They say it will be a boy."

"They told our fathers you and I would be boys too."

She shrugged. "Thank you for coming to see me. Now I must practice more."

So formal! Well, we had all changed in the last few weeks. I bade her luck with her archery and made my way back to the house.

By the end of the week they were both gone: Sir Thomas to London, and Elizabeth off with her household and yeomen of the guard for Hatfield.

We parted friends, all of us. Yet a cold hand lay upon the house, and it made me shiver in fear.

Katharine came down with a cold. It rained steadily. She took to her bed and I read to her for hours. Greek mythology. She loved it. Also some Latin. But inside me my heart ached. For I blamed myself, just as Sir Thomas had blamed me. If only I had kept my mouth shut. Now our family was broken up, and I had a bad feeling about things to come.

I helped Katharine fit out the nursery. Oh, it was to be beautiful. The walls were hung with blue silk at Sir Thomas's request.

But Katharine insisted on some pink pillows. "Just in case it's a girl," she said.

The cradle was draped in silk. Draperies hung like ladies' skirts at the windows. The bed for the nurse was swathed in crimson. Would Sir Thomas be back in time for the baby's birth? A midwife was engaged.

"If I were Queen," Katharine told me, "I would have to take to my private chambers a month ahead of time and not be seen. How tiresome to be Queen. Don't ever let them make you Queen, Jane." She clutched my hand tightly, saying it. Was her hand warm? Was she feverish?

Two days later Sir Thomas returned, laden with gifts for us and for the new baby. And the house came alive again with his voice, his step, his laughter. His presence dismissed all my ghosts. No one dared be grave with Sir Thomas around.

I knew why Elizabeth had been in love with him and felt ashamed of myself even thinking it. I adored him, in spite of everything, and knew it to be a weakness in myself that I must conquer.

But he thought of me still as a child, for his gift to me was a doll. I smiled and thanked him. He was solemn with me, and proper, but oh how I longed to have my old Sir Thomas back. Time was he'd take me on his lap and count the freckles on my nose.

A whole month he'd been gone, and still I knew he had not forgiven me. Would he ever?

Katharine was delivered of a baby girl on August thirtieth. The midwife's name was Maude, and she kept Katharine entertained while the baby was coming with tales of how she had delivered the Princess Elizabeth and how frightened she'd been to tell King Henry that he had a daughter, not a son.

"I thought he was going to have me head then and there," she said.

And when the baby finally came she held it up and pronounced: "I tell you as I told the King then. You have a beautiful baby girl."

Katherine was smiling even as tears came down her face. "Where is my husband?" she asked.

The baby was beautiful. But so small! How could a body be so small and survive? I wondered at the miracle of it. I couldn't stop staring at her, and when the midwife offered to let me hold the baby, I declined.

Sir Thomas came in, hesitant in this women's realm, cautious and not at all disappointed. He kissed Katharine tenderly, inquired after her health, and held the baby. Sir Thomas seemed enamored of the child.

People came to visit in great plenty and filed right through Katharine's chambers with gifts the next few days, as was the custom. She received them sitting up in bed with her beautiful hair down around her shoulders, wearing her silken gown, and Sir Thomas poured the wine and

I gave out the sweetmeats.

For three days the house was in a cocoon of happiness. Then Katharine took sick with fever. The doctor was called in by a worried Sir Thomas.

It was childbed fever. For two days she tossed and turned in delirium, and I seldom left her side. Oh, how frightened I was. Most women with childbed fever died of it. But surely Katharine would not die! Surely the Good Lord was not that cruel. I clung to her hand. I never left her bed and had to be told to go and get some sleep.

Whenever Sir Thomas came in, I was there. We spoke little. She accused him once of poisoning her, of wanting her dead, of wanting her money, and I flinched for him, seeing the look on his face.

"You never loved me," she accused him.

"I always loved you, sweetheart."

"You love that Elizabeth. That Boleyn brat."

"You are my wife. You have my heart."

On the third day her delirium ceased, and she sat up and called for her secretary and pen and paper and made up her will, leaving everything to Sir Thomas.

That night she died.

I was with her, as was Sir Thomas. I saw the life go out of her body, something I had never witnessed before. It appalled me. Surely I could not bear it if she left us. She had been the center of my world. What would I do without her? I refused to believe she was gone. They had to lead me away from her bed.

I saw Sir Thomas lean over her and clutch her hand and weep, his whole body shaking.

"Sir Thomas . . ." I tried to comfort him. I put my hand on his arm.

He raised his head. "Get out of here," he demanded, "now. You helped sow the mistrust in her for me. Leave now."

It was worse than being slapped. I backed out of the room, telling myself his grief was speaking, not he. But I knew what my feelings of doom had been for. Were we all doomed, then? Was there to be no happiness on this earth for any of us?

Sir Thomas mourned, locking himself away in his study. But first he sent for me.

I braced myself for more scolding, more recriminations. But it was not to be. It was as if the scene in Katharine's chambers had never happened. He was completely becalmed. "Jane, I wish you to be chief mourner. Can you do this for me?"

"Yes, sir." I felt a rush of joy.

"And I wish you to write to Elizabeth and tell her. Will you do that?"

I would do anything, but I simply said "Yes, sir" again.

I'd been crying, and he saw it. "Don't cry, Jane. She is in heaven."

"But she is all I had on this earth," I sobbed. "All who loved me."

"You are loved, Jane," he said quietly. "But you are too good, that is your problem. The rest of us aren't. We are simply human. And you bring us to task by your very presence."

"I don't mean to be that way, sir."

"Then don't be. I'm inviting my mother to come and stay. To keep the household together and make it a proper one. I expect your father to write and demand you come home now, since it is not a proper household anymore. But I shall not give you up. I go this afternoon to see the King. Edward. Is there anything you wish, Jane?"

"Take me with you."

"No. You are chief mourner. Remember your duties."

"Yes, sir."

He left. And again the world went cold.

~TEN~

To be chief mourner was an honor, and I tried to remind myself of that as I sat in the chapel with Katharine's body deep into the night while people came and went.

I was not afraid to be alone with her coffin. There were many candles, and the people who came were so many that I scarce had time to think. I must greet them for Sir Thomas. I must wear long black robes and welcome everyone. I must listen to the sermon next day, by a Mr. Coverdale, who had translated the Bible into English. I must be first in line to follow the corpse to the grave.

But I could not believe they were taking my Katharine to the grave. She had been so alive, so warm, so dear, and now she was snuffed out like a candle. I could not accept that.

They named the baby Mary and a special nurse was brought in to see to her, but Sir Thomas seemed not to have too much interest in the child.

A note did come around from my father to Sir Thomas, expressing his concern because it was "not a proper household anymore." He wanted me home.

To make it proper, Sir Thomas did indeed send for his mother, and she came.

She was a small lady of ancient age, with white hair, and for some reason I was surprised to see how tender he was with her.

"I know you will love Jane as if she were my daughter," he said to her. And I felt that mayhap part of him, at least, had forgiven me.

And so it became a proper household again. People came and went; I did my studies and played my music. And I sewed with old Lady Seymour. She told me stories of Sir Thomas and Sir Edward when they were boys. "They would kill each other if left alone in a room together," she said.

Then she told me of another son, who never went to court, who was forty now and whose name was Sir Henry. "He doesn't fancy power or glitter," she said. "He stays to himself. He's a farmer, a country squire."

"Thomas, being the younger, is a loveable rogue," she said, "but Edward is too serious in his role of Protector.

"Did I ever tell you of the day King Henry stopped at

our house and first met my daughter, Jane? Oh, he was taken with her, I tell you.

"I think Thomas sees much of her in you," she told me.

"I am afraid he is displeased with me," I confessed.

"He's displeased with himself these days. Don't let his abruptness hurt you. He has lost his wife and is having dealings with men I do not consider honest. He resents the power his brother has over King Edward, and I am afraid he would do anything to topple him."

"Anything?"

She shook her head and put her finger over her lips.

She told me how her daughter Jane had attended the beehives at home, how she took care of the linen and the flower garden. "She was a good girl," she said. "And now here is Thomas with both his sister and his wife dying in childbirth. Be patient with him."

She was. She made no complaint when Thomas had his "men visitors," who came on beautiful horses with gentlemen-in-waiting, and drank wine and ate far into the night. I glimpsed them once in the dining room. They seemed to be plotting by candlelight. They whispered. They mumbled. They roared with laughter, and Thomas one of them. I heard talk of ships and ports and cargo and money.

And then too he was away a lot. Once when he was away, the other brother came around—Sir Henry. He came on a good horse but he came alone, no gentlemen-in-waiting, no retinue of eager young men.

75

He was a likeable man, affable, benign of countenance, concerned about animals and the hay in the fields. He smiled at me and called me lovely. "My little brother has all the luck," he said.

But at supper he made no effort to keep it from me as he told his mother how worried he was about Thomas.

He spoke of a castle in Cheshire that Thomas owned, that he was shoring up in case of revolt. Of a trip Thomas had made to Boulogne to see to defenses there. About his mustering a small army in hopes of displacing Edward as Protector. Of his wanting to marry Elizabeth right after Katharine's death.

I shivered at such talk. Was Sir Thomas truly so reckless? I knew that if these things were so, he was playing with fire.

"Talk to him, Mama," Sir Henry said. "He creates his own destruction."

The months went on until summer became winter. Sir Thomas came and went. I scarcely saw him even when he was home, although I would see him on occasion in the front hallway when I was coming in and he was going out.

"How are your studies?"

"Fine, sir."

"I've spoken with your tutor. He says your Greek could be better."

"He is mad over Greek."

"So should you be."

And he'd be off, riding through the fallen leaves that were on the ground, on his handsome horse with his retinue of men.

That winter there were rumors—stories that seemed to spring up from the frozen ground. How could the same stories, the same rumors that were in London, travel out here?

I was in the barn one day when I overheard one stableboy telling another:

"A midwife, a wise woman, was wakened one night last September by a horseman wearing a green velvet mask. He bade her mount the horse he brought, put a blindfold over her eyes, and brought her to a place in the forest. The house was large and she was brought through many rooms. Then finally they removed the blindfold, and she found herself in a room richly furnished, and on the bed lay a young maid in labor. Her hair was rich and red. And she brought forth a babe that the masked man took from her and carried out into the night and gave to a waiting couple.

"The midwife was paid in gold. And told never to speak of what she had seen and done this night. And she was taken home. And there are those who say the mother of the child is the Princess Elizabeth, and the house was Hatfield. Yes."

I froze hearing that. Could it be true? Did such things truly happen on God's good earth? I knew that rumors spread like the plague during the long English winters. People were bored and told stories around the fire. But this! It made me angry, but I could do nothing. To deny it would only give it more life. I tried to forget and hoped it would go away.

There are rumors that are soon forgotten, and those that take on a life of their own and become more true than truth.

For such a rumor was Sir Thomas taken.

It was February, snow was falling, and inside Chelsea Manor all was warm and comfortable and safe when the horseman rode up that day.

There was a rattling at the front door. A manservant went to open it, and in they stepped, men who said they came in the name of King Edward.

I hear the words still. "Sir Thomas, you are under arrest for treason and murder." The words were like cannonballs hurled into our quietude that day, but Sir Thomas only laughed, called for his cloak, and kissed his mother, who was walking around the men folding and unfolding her hands and crying.

"Don't cry, Mother. I'll be back before nightfall."

"Not likely," one of the men said.

"Not from the Tower," another put in.

I was trembling. What was all this about. Murder? Treason? My cousin Edward had ordered this? Or was this the work of the Lord Protector, Sir Thomas's own brother? I thought again of the rumor spoken by the stableboy.

I looked at him. "Sir Thomas," I said.

But he was giving some instructions to his mother.

"Sir Thomas," I said again, and he looked at me then, but he did not say any soft words, or comforting ones, or even gallant ones.

"Take care of my mother," he admonished me.

So he *never* had forgiven me, never, for my telling Katharine the things I told her. And I knew, as I watched him go out the door, that he never would.

~ ELEVEN ~

Our days of anguish became a week, then two. Lady Seymour was distraught. She had no hope and kept talking about how her son Edward, the Protector, had always wanted his brother Sir Thomas out of the way. "I saw my daughter Jane wed King Henry and die when she gave birth to the boy king," she said continually. "I am grandmother to the boy king who has signed an arrest warrant for Sir Thomas, his favorite uncle. And I should have hope?"

"Why has the little king done this?" she would ask me. "Why?"

Why, indeed? I longed to go and see him, but could not leave the distraught Lady Seymour. Then help arrived in the person of Sir Henry, come for a visit.

He stayed two days, and his presence in the house was like a breath of spring air.

He came, he said, to see his mother again, to comfort her, to try to make inquiries about why Sir Thomas was being held. "They aren't giving him a trial," he said. "There's mischief afoot. It turns out my brother was mustering an army to overcome Sir Edward as Protector," he told his mother. "That's the treason part of it."

"The murder part" he spoke of was the rumor that took on a life of its own and became people's truth. "They are saying that he poisoned Katharine."

There, I thought, *there is the reason the King signed his arrest warrant.* Young Edward had always loved Katharine. He considered her his second mother. Either that, or Edward, his Protector, had convinced him to sign the warrant. Oh, had the young King changed so much since I last saw him? Or was he unduly influenced? I must find out!

Sir Henry and his mother talked and planned. He would go to Sir Edward, the Lord Protector, he said. As the eldest brother he'd give him a piece of his mind. What did he mean by sending men around to arrest their brother in front of their mother like that?

When I saw him making ready for the trip, I begged to go. "Take me, Sir Henry. I can talk to the King. We are friends."

He was a kindly man of medium height and no dash or flair like Sir Thomas, but his kindness was real. And his eyes knew things I wished Sir Thomas's eyes had known.

"His brother will put Thomas to death," was all Lady Seymour would say.

"No brother will ever put another to death," Henry tried to reassure us.

But I don't think he believed it.

"The people don't like it," Henry told me, "that Sir Thomas was arrested in front of his mother and his ward, a slip of a girl. You can get away with so much as a nobleman. But the people mark what you do. Even King Henry kept his eye on the feelings of the people. They rise up if they don't like something, and they don't like these doings with Tom."

We were on our way to London.

"He has an eye for you, hey?" he said of King Edward. "Tom always said he would wed you to him."

I liked Sir Henry. I felt at ease with him.

"Yes, he has an eye for me," I said. "And I for him."

"Then mayhap he'll give Tom a trial. There are thirty-three charges of treason against him. They aren't planning on giving him a trial. They talk of a Bill of Attainder. Under it the person is not allowed to speak in his own defense. What rot. The Council questioned him in the Tower. Plain rot. Edward didn't even go."

"Your mother says Sir Thomas undermines Sir Edward's authority," I told him. "That Sir Thomas has been plotting against Sir Edward for the past two years. And that it will now be the death of one or the other. Do you think she is right?" My voice shook.

"Don't listen to my mother," he told me.

I found Edward, the King, in his privy chamber under the royal canopy. In front of him on the table was a chessboard, and he was moving the figures on it around and around, all by himself.

Behind him sun streamed through a stained-glass window, making shafts of color near his chair.

"Edward."

He looked up. "Jane, my friend! What a surprise! Come to me!"

I would have run, that was my first impulse, but I stopped myself and walked decorously to where he sat and knelt. "My liege," I said.

"No, Jane, no, don't kneel. We're alone. I don't often get the chance to be alone, but they told me you were here and so I sent them all away. Come, give me a hug."

I stood up and embraced him. His shoulders were still thin—he was still a little boy. And his face looked pale and wan.

"Edward, I've come to beg you for something," I said.

"I know, I know. Don't sign the death warrant for Sir Tom. He's my uncle, Jane; do you think I am fain to sign it? I have always loved Uncle Thomas. He was good to me."

"Then why do it?"

"Because I am King, and it is what kings do. It has not been easy, Jane. I hate being King most of the time. But it is what I must do."

"The Lord Protector tells you this."

"He advises me, yes. He fears his brother. Thirty-three charges of treason are serious business, Jane. Uncle Thomas was forming an army to march against us."

"Not you. If he was planning anything, it was against his brother."

"It's the same thing."

"How will you feel afterward, signing a death warrant for one you love?"

"He poisoned Katharine. Everyone knows it."

"I don't know it and I was there. The whole time, I was there. He loved Katharine."

"He wants to wed my sister Elizabeth."

"He never said such to me. Or his mother. Rumors, talk, all of it. A man should not die for rumors."

"And what of the story going around about the midwife and the man in the velvet mask?" he asked.

"Oh, Edward, don't believe that. You know how people get in England in the middle of winter."

He looked at me. His face was pinched and white. "I'm sorry, Jane. You don't know how sorry I am."

He hugged me. And we cried together. And I thought, *I will never be Queen, never. If the time ever comes, I will throw the crown at them all.*

TWELVE

They beheaded Sir Thomas Seymour, Lord High Admiral of England, on Tower Hill on a cold day in March 1549.

King Edward signed the death warrant.

Sir Thomas's own brother let it happen. He did nothing to stop it and he could have. He could have spoken soft words to the little king about his Uncle Thomas. He could have imprisoned Sir Thomas for a while in the Tower, until all was quiet again in the kingdom.

He could have remembered that Sir Thomas was his younger brother or recalled old times at home, or even done it in the name of King Edward's mother, their sister Jane.

He did none of these things, and so they cut off the

head of the man who, in Princess Elizabeth's words, "was wonderful but not too wise."

And true to Sir Henry's words, the people were not happy that the Lord Protector should allow his own brother to go to his death. The Lord Protector was losing his popularity.

To further their discontent there were other troubles: workmen without work, bad harvests the previous fall, and too many changes in religious beliefs. The people did not like changes and tended to blame their troubles on the ruling class.

My parents summoned me home. I left Lady Seymour with a heavy heart and went back to Bradgate. I would never believe that Sir Thomas was guilty of all those charges of treason. And I knew he hadn't poisoned Katharine.

Going home, after living away, was difficult enough. When I got there, I discovered that my parents had betrothed me to the Protector's son Edward, the Earl of Hertford.

"Why?" I asked.

"Because there is no more chance, with Sir Thomas dead, of your marrying the King," my father admitted. "This will be a good match for you. You have met the younger Seymour, haven't you?"

"Yes, Father."

"And how do you think of him?"

"I don't like his father, but of him I think well enough."

"So then, you are betrothed."

I was eleven, going on twelve. When a girl was fourteen she was considered a woman. Truth to tell, I did not wish to be betrothed to anybody, but I knew there was no sense in protesting. As for love, how could I love anybody? I had loved King Edward. I still did. I had loved Sir Thomas. Not the way Elizabeth had professed to love him, no. My love was not dangerous. But it was genuine.

The only good thing about being in my home was that it was big enough for me to hide from my family during the day. And I needed to hide from my mother. For I was in disgrace since Sir Thomas's death. Even though they'd betrothed me to the Earl of Hertford, they were still disappointed that I couldn't wed King Edward.

I was a big disappointment to them. And they treated me with disdain because of it.

Mother questioned me constantly about Chelsea Manor, about life there, about Katharine's death. "Do you think he poisoned her?"

"No, Mother."

"Well, everyone says so. How could you have allowed such a thing to happen? You were there. Didn't you see?"

"I saw nothing. And he didn't poison her. Please don't disparage his name. He's dead."

For which I was slapped. "And this business with the Princess Elizabeth. Is it true. Did he flirt with her in her bedroom?"

"It was all in good fun. Katharine was there." I lied for Sir Thomas. It was the very least I could do for him, to stop his name from being dragged through the mud.

"Oh, get out of my sight. I send you to live with the Queen Dowager and the brother of the Lord Protector and you can't even do it right."

And so I ran to my chambers, where my sister Catherine found me an hour or so later, hugging Pourquoi. "Jane, Jane, you'll never guess what."

"What is it, Catherine?"

"I'm betrothed!"

She was not yet ten. And she stood there in front of me, her gold hair around her shoulders, her blue eyes sparkling. Already she conducted herself like a woman, and being the prettier, found favor over me with Mother.

"To whom?"

"Henry Herbert, son of the Earl of Pembroke. And he's as dashing as your earl."

"I'm glad for you, Catherine. That's quite a match."

"You must tell me. How does one act when one is betrothed?"

"Much the same as you act now."

"Am I allowed to kiss him?" She giggled.

"It's only a formality, Catherine. And it can be broken off in an instant, and likely will be, if his fortunes change."

"Mother and Father are intent on having us all betrothed. They're planning now for Mary. They want her betrothed by the end of the month."

"Mary? No. She's not . . ." My voice failed. I thought of Mary, poor little hunchback Mary. She was just a child!

"Mother says she is most suitable. And you'd best not object, Jane."

"What's all the commotion I heard below?"

"There is more news. Mother's half brothers have both been killed in a terrible accident. They drowned crossing the channel on a ship in a storm."

"She never liked them. Is she distraught?"

Catherine giggled. "As distraught as anybody would be who has just inherited a title. Father is now Duke of Suffolk. A courier just arrived. They've got all kinds of money and new lands and castles."

I ran back downstairs. They were in Father's library, poring over legal papers. "You can't. You can't betroth Mary," I cried. "Please don't, she is such a shy child. She—"

"How dare you break in here and accost us like this?" Mother stood up. "Your father is now the Duke of Suffolk. Have a little more respect, please."

I curtsied low. "I'm sorry, Father, but I worry about Mary."

"Do you think we don't know what is best for her? You

presume too much, Jane. Since you have returned from Chelsea Manor, you just presume too much."

I started to sob. They would sell Mary off like a horse, to align themselves with some other vein of royalty.

"Stop that blubbering," Mother ordered. "What they did to you at Chelsea Manor, I don't know. I think you are due for a visit with Princess Mary. She always has a sobering effect on you."

That's right. Ship me off again to someone else, I thought. And when I come back they'll have my little sister Mary betrothed to some Irish nobleman, and she'll have to go off to live on the wild bogs and swamps of Ireland. Oh, I hated them both so much. How I missed Katharine and Sir Thomas.

As it turned out, I stayed at home for many long, dismal months. There was nothing dismal about Bradgate itself. Now that Father was Duke of Suffolk and Mother was Duchess, they put on all kinds of entertainments. There were always plenty of people around, houseguests who never seemed to go home, huntsmen with their grand horses and green livery. There were nights when it was difficult to sleep for the noise that came from belowstairs, where my parents partied and gambled. And they hired the best for their parties. They hired drummers and pipers, Master John Heywood's troupe of child performers, Lord Russell's minstrels.

Sometimes the house was so full of people, you didn't know who you were bumping into in the receiving room, grand hall, or galleries. The stables were overflowing too, and I came to prefer to saddle my own horse rather than wait my turn for a groom to do it for me.

My father held many jousting tournaments. I did like to watch these from the pavilion in the tilting yard. It was exciting, seeing the knights charging at each other in all their armor, their horses snorting and garbed in all the trappings of the event.

We played our parts, my sisters and I, handing our silk kerchiefs over to the knights just before the joust. They would stuff them inside their breastplates and go to take their positions.

There was one knight who always won in these tournaments, even against my father, who was an expert jouster. I didn't know who he was, but one day while I was holding out my silk kerchief, he rode up to where I sat in the pavilion, dipped his lance in salute, and said, "Ah, the Lady Jane. May I have the token of your affection, then, and ride into battle with it?"

My sister Catherine, sitting next to me, nudged me and whispered, "Say yes; it's Northumberland."

I handed over my silk kerchief. Expertly he lifted it with the end of his lance, stuffed it in his breastplate, and rode off on his magnificent charger.

"Who is he?" I asked Catherine.

"He comes here often. You'd better be nice to him. His father is our father's dear friend. Lord High Admiral, Master of the Horse, Viscount Lisle, and the father of thirteen children."

"I don't like his eyes. Why did he come to me like that?"

"I don't know, but I've heard him and Father discussing you."

Sweet Lord. What did they have planned for me now?

In that year King Edward came down with the measles and everyone became very nervous. I wanted to go and visit him, but my parents refused, lest I catch the measles and bring them home. I worried for Edward. He wasn't strong to begin with.

Those who had much to gain by who was on the throne began visiting Princess Mary at Beaulieu, her country seat, presenting themselves to her, thinking she would soon be Queen.

Oh, the monstrous duplicity of people!

I objected when my parents insisted I go to visit Mary. "It will only remind her there are people in line for the throne after her," I said.

But I must go, I was told. There was nothing for it. I hated it because I would not have Mary think me an opportunist. But I went anyway.

∼THIRTEEN∼

S o the spring I was fifteen I paid another visit to Mary.
And I couldn't help but notice. She treated me like
a woman now.

"You know John Dudley, the Duke of Northumberland,
of course," she said to me as soon as we were seated in comfort in her private chambers. "What do you know about
him?"

"That I like him not," I said.

She smiled. Mary was well past thirty now, with the
flush of maidenhood gone from her face. But then, had she
ever been a true maid? All her life she had had to act with
wisdom beyond her years just to survive.

I was glad I wasn't a princess. Their lot is not a
happy one.

"You should not only like him not," she told me. "You should fear him. He is not a man of good parts. He may be elegant, handsome, and accomplished, but it is he who set the Seymour brothers against each other. And now he is working to upset the Lord Protector."

"How?" I asked.

"For one thing, Northumberland has just put down a bothersome rebellion. Everyone praises him for it. Few stop to think it gave him an excuse to have his own army, and now that he does, the Lord Protector is in danger of being thrown over."

"Will King Edward allow that to happen?"

"My little brother is enamored of Northumberland. You know he's the finest jouster of the day and has a skill at games that fascinates Edward. He treats my brother as if he has already attained his majority. And he has hangers-on and climbers in court who will falsely testify in a minute to the Lord Protector's treasonous activities."

Fear came upon me. "And if he takes over as Lord Protector?"

"You and I are both in danger. You'll find yourself no longer betrothed to your earl, but likely to one of Northumberland's sons. He has five of them. You know your parents want you attached to power."

"I can't think of one I'd want to be betrothed to."

"No matter. One is already wed. Prepare yourself for it, though. "

"And you?" I looked at her. She was no longer pretty, no, but there was a certain strength in her face. And honesty. With herself.

"All the council is with him," she said of Northumberland. "Including Cranmer, Wriothesley, Arundel, Paulet, and Cecil. I am friendly with the council, but if Northumberland takes over, I shall have to flee England."

I leaned forward. "Where would you go?"

"Portugal. I am thinking Portugal," she said.

She was lying to herself now. For even I knew they would never let her out of England. A princess of the blood in a foreign country? With the opportunity to mass an army around her and return and attack and take over the throne? No, she was surely lying to herself now.

"Are you going to the reception for Mary, Queen of Guise?" she asked me.

Mary, Queen of Guise was Queen Regent of Scotland, returning to her homeland after a trip. "I don't know," I said.

"You must, if just to see Edward. He's had the measles, you know, and we've all been worried about him."

"Are you going?"

"No. It's too dangerous for me at court. And I'll wager Elizabeth doesn't go, either. But here, I have a present for you." She clapped her hands and one of her ladies-in-waiting brought over a dress, and Mary held it across her lap.

"You must go. And wear this. For me."

It was made of tinsel cloth of gold and velvet, laid on with parchment lace of gold. She then reached into a box on a side table and drew out a pearl-and-ruby necklace, and bade me try it on. So I did.

The red ruby drops drew close around my throat in the fashion of the time.

"I can't take these things, Mary," I said.

"You can and you shall. If I know your parents, they won't dress you properly. And you are so pretty, Jane, and deserve to look like a princess in your own right."

We kissed. She was good to me and we chatted longer, sharing secrets, and I felt a warmth inside me I hadn't felt since Katharine was alive.

"No reason we can't be like sisters," she said. "We must help each other against the common enemy."

Beaulieu, her country seat, was a beautiful place, a stone mansion with three turrets, a wonderful cherry orchard, streams, and well-ordered gardens and stables. Not only that, but Mary had her own household here, maids and grooms, her own chaplain who said mass daily in the beautiful chapel.

Inside the house were a grand staircase, handsome furniture, carpets from Turkey, paintings, draperies from Florence. But still, I felt sorry for Mary. She was still an outlander here, far from court, although it did seem that she had her spies to keep her informed.

She would be Queen someday. I was sure of it. But when I left, I envied her not.

The reception for Mary, Queen of Guise, was held in the enormous hall of Westminster Palace. There were enough tables to serve five hundred, tables set with white linen and gold plate. The season's plenty was served, everything from huge platters of spiced pork and roast swans to special iced cakes made in the shapes of all the King's palaces.

The Master of the Revels had designed a special entertainment. King Edward loved entertainments almost as much as his father had. And though pale, he was recovered from the measles, for which I was most relieved and thankful. How good to see him up and about again. After the entertainment there was dancing.

Had I not trusted Mary, I would have said she gave me the dress to put me in a better light with Guildford Dudley, son of Northumberland. For that is exactly what happened at the reception. Everyone complimented me on the dress, on how lovely I looked, until I wanted to hide in a far corner of the room, behind the music players.

"You look so beautiful, Jane. I'm so proud to be betrothed to you," Edward said as he led me out to dance.

Mayhap it was because my Edward was shy, besides being good looking, that I liked him. I did not love him, no.

I did not expect to love him right off in the beginning. Love would come later, I was told. Since our betrothal he had sent around gifts for me, mostly books, which he knew I liked. He was tender and sweet, and I felt safe and even saucy dancing with him.

But then Guildford Dudley came over and took my hand. "May I have the honor?" he asked.

Guildford was fair, unlike his dark-haired brothers, John, Henry, Ambrose, and Robert. I had heard they were a close family, that they never fought or even disagreed, that there was perfect harmony in the Northumberland house.

It made me suspicious. Nobody had perfect harmony in his house. And if he did, it was because one member held sway over the others, and of course I knew the "one" was Northumberland, their father.

"I'm dancing with Edward, my betrothed," I told Guildford. "You know Edward. His father is Lord Protector."

"You know what my father says," Guildford said. "Out of twelve who kneel, seven would willingly cut the throats of both the King and the Duke of Somerset."

"You speak treason, surely."

He smiled, as he insinuated himself between us and smoothly guided me into the dance, leaving Edward open-mouthed on the sidelines.

"What mean you by that?" I asked him when the

dance brought us close together.

"That you might think on it and decide you'd like to be betrothed to the son of him who will soon be the real Lord Protector."

"I don't decide to whom I wish to be betrothed," I snapped.

"Pity. I do." And he glided with me through the steps of the dance as if he'd been born to it.

"You know, my grandmother, Elizabeth de Lisle, is a descendant of Warwick the King-Maker," he told me as we danced.

"And your mother?"

"A delightful lady, I am sure."

"I hear she spoils you, that you run to her every time you can't get what you want."

"I am her favorite, yes."

"And so? What is that to me?"

"Mull it over, Lady Jane. You do look lovely in that dress. Like a princess in your own right."

"I have no desire to look like a princess," I said.

"A queen mayhap?" And he laughed. There was something maniacal in the laugh, I decided, but of course I kept up the pretense. To do anything less would be an insult to everyone assembled. But before the evening was over, I had decided that Guildford Dudley, though fair of hair and blue of eye and one of the handsomest men in the room, was a stuffed prig. And I would never be betrothed to him. Never.

The next day was Saint George's Day, the twenty-third of April, so there was a special service in Westminster Abbey. I went. King Edward looked so very small and so very far away from me, taking part, wearing his heavy velvet Garter robes. I thought he looked lost in them.

Afterward I was able to see him alone—something I hadn't been able to do the previous night.

"How are you, my liege?" I asked.

"If you don't call me Edward, I'll have you put in the Tower," he joked.

He made me smile. "Are you truly well now?" I asked.

"I'm in fine fettle."

"I'm so glad of your good escape out of the perilous disease."

"I've been tilting at the quintain, running at the ring, hawking, and I am going this afternoon on a trip on my royal barge down the river."

"Don't take on too much."

"Tomorrow I attend a goodly muster of my men-at-arms. And tonight we're having acrobats and high-wire artists perform."

"And then there are your public duties," I said.

"Yes. Next week I must inspect the naval dockyard at

Portsmouth. And in June I go on my Progress. I'm riding all through London and touring my entire kingdom. We'll put up at the houses of the great nobles all along the route in the southern and western counties."

"It's too much of a schedule for you, Edward. Who says you can do all this?"

He leaned close to me. "Northumberland. I like the man. He doesn't coddle me, but treats me as if I've already come into a man's estate."

Oh, I wanted to tell him to beware. But one did not say such things to a king.

⌒ FOURTEEN ⌒

I was still living at home, which was, in comparison to court life, quiet and countrified. In spite of my parents' lavish entertainments, there were quiet days that pleased me, days without revelry and games and jousts.

So being home was not all bad. I spent time with my tutor, whom I liked, and my sisters, whom I liked on occasion. I rode my horse and I wandered about the place at will.

I liked, best, to wander around the farm part of the manor. There were all sorts of wonderful things to see, the chickens and roosters in their pens, the sheep, the cows and their calves. Everything about the farm was orderly, thanks to Drumson, who ran it for Father. He was interested in roosters, in breeding new types, and I'd go to see what new birds he had in his cages.

On one particular spring morning I was admiring a rather cocky fellow who was new, when Drumson and I both looked up toward the front of the house. A thundering of hooves announced a whole party of men who came into the courtyard and dismounted. Their colors were green and white. And there were at least twelve yeomen of the guard.

"Looks like you have an important visitor, Lady Jane," Drumson said, half in jest. Everything he said was half in jest. "Mayhap you'd best get into the house and see."

"I'll stay here," I said.

I went on to the buttery, where Sally and Margret were just putting a crock of cream into a churn. Sometimes they'd let me have a go at it. I loved churning butter, though I swore them to secrecy. Mother would have beaten me if she'd seen me doing it.

I didn't ask to churn that morning, though. Truth to tell, I was hiding. I did not know from what, but I knew I had to hide as long as I could.

I hid in the buttery, listening to the chatter of Sally and Margret, until a whole churn of butter was finished, and until the swarm of men had departed. When that happened, I heard my name from a page, likely sent to find me.

"Lady Jane! Lady Jane, are you in there? Your mother wants you. Now!"

Margret gave me a taste of the newly made butter. I pronounced it the best I'd ever tasted and then went out to answer the page's call.

"We are breaking your troth to Edward," my mother told me. "Henceforth you are betrothed to Lord Guildford Dudley."

I felt as if they'd thrown cold water into my face. "Northumberland's son! But why?"

"He is the better match," Mother said.

"How so?" I demanded. "He's conceited and spoiled."

So they told me how so. "The Lord Protector is no longer in power. He's been accused of treason and conspiracy. He's been sent to the Tower."

I had no reply. It did not surprise me. Nor did their decision.

"He's been accused of wanting to take control of the kingdom. Of wanting to poison the entire council at a state banquet."

"I've always known him for a schemer. He put his own brother to death. But I don't trust Northumberland, either," I told them.

"Just because you were at court, doesn't mean you know things," my mother scolded. "You're still a child. And as such, will obey your parents."

"I won't be betrothed to Guildford Dudley. He's despicable."

"He's handsome, gallant, and respectful to his elders. He and all his brothers are loyal to their father in every way. You could do worse."

"I won't!" I stamped my foot then, a childish reaction. But Father would have none of it.

"You'll do as you're told, Jane."

"I don't love him."

He laughed. "Love! You know better than to use that argument with me. Love has naught to do with it. Anyway, you will come to love him. Northumberland was just here. He wants you for his son. And we have promised."

"You had no right."

"Don't sass us, girl. Or I'll have you beaten."

"Beat me. I don't care!"

My father's voice softened. "You are fond of your cousin, Lord Grey de Wilton?"

"Of course. He's a dear gentle young man. Why can't I be betrothed to him?"

"Because we are thinking of him for your sister Mary. You would approve of that?"

"If Mary must be betrothed, yes. He's always been good to her."

"We are also thinking of Lord Constance for her."

"That fat old prig? Never!"

"Do as you're told, then, and your sister will be betrothed to Lord Grey de Wilton."

I felt everything inside me drop onto the cold dank

floor that my soul had become. Betrothed to Guildford Dudley to save Mary? They knew I would. And oh, I hated them for the conceit of their knowing, for their manipulation of me. For making me so trapped. I felt like a fox in a leg trap.

Tears came into my eyes. But I fought them. I'd not cry. I'd not give them the satisfaction. *Oh, Sir Thomas, where are you?* I cried inside. *Queen Katharine, why did you have to die?*

"Has a date been set for my marriage?" I asked dismally. I couldn't bear the thought of it.

"The twenty-first of May," my father said.

One month away!

"And it is your sister Catherine's wedding day also. To Lord Henry Herbert, the eldest son of the Earl of Pembroke. We have done well for all our girls. What say you, Jane?"

"You aren't marrying Mary that day, are you?"

Father had the decency to look embarrassed. "No. She can wait a bit. Well, what say you?"

"Nothing," I said. I knew there was nothing I could say that would matter. So why bother?

Father laughed. "It's like a knife in the breast to have a thankless child," he said. And I was dismissed.

I would write to King Edward, that's what I would do. I would tell him of the outrageous demands of my parents.

I would have him forbid the match.

I did, but he did not reply. And so I knew my letter, and the next one, were kept from him. The boy king would never ignore a letter from me—he would, even if there was nothing he could do, reply. But he did not.

Rumors were rife that King Edward was not well, that he was failing. Now he had the smallpox. I knew I had to see him, especially if he was ill, so I decided to approach my father. And so, amidst all the hasty preparations for Catherine's and my upcoming weddings, I thought about how best to do it.

One did not approach Father for a favor unless one was willing to render a favor. Like my agreeing to be betrothed to Dudley to have Mary betrothed to Lord Grey de Wilton, everything was done in the bargaining style.

I decided to promise not to mention the matter of my betrothal, if I was just permitted to see Edward. And Father agreed to it. He was so happy that he was shortly to marry off two daughters, that I should have pushed for more. He might have agreed to anything.

I found King Edward shockingly ill the day I finally got to see him. He was recovered from the smallpox but coughed constantly.

"Only a few minutes," Northumberland said as he ushered me into the presence chamber. "He is weak."

I sat on a chair next to the throne where Edward insisted on sitting, though he was slumped over. He seemed feverish. What looked to be bruises were like half moons under his eyes, and his face was pinched as he tried not to cough in front of me.

Fear ran all through me. Wasn't there something they could do for him?

"The Italian doctor is here. He will make me well," he said. And he gestured with his head to a far corner of the room, where a man dressed in black was bent over a desk working on something.

"Dr. Cardano," Edward told me.

"What is he doing?"

"Casting my horoscope."

I drew in my breath. "But that is not allowed."

He smiled weakly. "I allow it. I just will not allow the results to be bandied about."

I wished Northumberland would leave us, but he would not. He must have sensed that I might ask Edward to forbid my marriage. But I had made a promise to my father not to ask for that.

"So, you're to be married soon," Edward said with false brightness.

"Yes."

"I wish I could be there, Jane. But I dare not travel away from this palace."

"I know."

"I shall send gifts. The very best for you and your sister."

"Oh, Edward, my friend."

"Don't cry, Jane. You must be strong, for me. Promise me you will be strong for me."

I promised. And I hugged him when we parted, though I knew it was forbidden. Northumberland fair burst, watching us. He was pacing back and forth. "Come now, come, don't tire His Majesty."

"Jane," he whispered to me, "I must sign Lord Somerset's death warrant. Northumberland tells me I must. I signed a death warrant for one uncle, I don't want to sign one for another, though he was accused of treason."

"What if you don't?" I asked him.

"There is no choice, Jane. Oh, how I hate being King."

Before I left, he had gifts brought forth by his servants. Costly jewels, cloth of gold and silver tissue for the wedding dresses, and many other rich clothes. A crown of gold and silver brocade for me to wear.

I burst into tears. "Oh, Edward, I can't leave you!"

We hugged again. If not for Northumberland, with his firm but kind orders, pulling us apart, I might never have left. "He needs his rest," he chided me gently. "Have your servants take the gifts, and know he'll be with you in spirit on your wedding day."

I was surprised at his kindness. I did not think the man had it in him. Some said his thoughts were all for the boy king, others said he was having him poisoned.

I left. In the gallery on the way out, I ran into Dr. Cardano. He nodded to me politely and stopped to talk. "What was in his horoscope?" I begged.

He shook his head sadly. "Ah, 'tis treason to predict the death of a king. All he needs is rest."

Half the people around Edward are lying, and the other half protecting themselves, I thought. How could he ever be well? There was no truth here. Look at Northumberland. He now owned three London palaces, two manor houses, and suites of rooms at Westminster and Whitehall. Why would *he* tell the truth?

I knew when I left that I would never see my cousin Edward again.

I knew that I could not believe any rumors or reports about him once I left the palace. That he could be dead two days and Northumberland would keep producing encouraging bulletins about his health.

It was not good when a king died. The people became frightened and restless. It was not good until another one was appointed in his place.

Only in this case, it would be a queen. Who? Mary, with her Catholic ways, undoing all my cousin Edward had done to make England a Protestant state? Elizabeth?

No, it had to be Mary. She was next in the line of succession. I did not envy her.

⌒ FIFTEEN ⌒

On the way out of the palace I met Princess Mary and her ladies-in-waiting in the great entranceway. And they were, indeed, waiting, as if for a royal barge to take them down the Thames.

She looked up when she saw me coming. "Jane!"

"Mary!"

We had never been as sisters as much as she liked to pretend, but now you would think we were. All our attendants stepped aside to give us our privacy. Mary put her arm around my shoulder. "I've been waiting and waiting to see him. They won't let me. Is he still alive, then?"

"Yes."

"And was he able to speak to you?"

"Yes."

"All I hear is wild rumors. He is dead, he is not dead. I will not wait another moment! I am the Princess! I am his sister!" Then softly: "How did you get in, Jane?"

I blushed. "Through my father." I hesitated, embarrassed. "Him and Northumberland."

"Ah yes, your father and Northumberland. They concoct all kinds of mischief between them. What happens when Edward dies, Jane?"

I lowered my head. "You are next in line for succession."

"Am I? Northumberland has been making overtures to me. Writing me letters, informing me of affairs of state and news of the court. Suggesting I again wear my family's coat of arms and giving me five hundred pounds to repair the dikes on my estate in Essex. Elizabeth has received nothing."

"He fears Elizabeth," I said.

"Still, I don't trust him. I think he is pacifying me. Oh, Jane, I must get into my brother's bedchamber. Will you help me?"

I was at a loss for what to do, when I turned and saw Dr. Cardano coming through the gallery. "This man can help you, I am sure. Dr. Cardano" — I reached out my hand — "please help Princess Mary get in to see her brother, won't you?"

He paused. With his black hood all but concealing his face, and his hands folded in front of him, he looked more like an executioner than a doctor. He bowed.

"Princess Mary," he said. "I am your humble servant."

"How is my brother?"

He shrugged.

"Dr. Cardano cast his horoscope," I said.

"Tell me," Mary ordered in a voice that had a good amount of queenly command. "Give me no false coin. Give me the truth."

I knew then that Edward was dying, because no one knew how to treat Mary. She could be queen tomorrow, or banished to the outlands. But here in court one did not take chances.

"I have seen the omens of a great calamity," Dr. Cardano said.

When I left, they were walking down the darkened gallery together, in the direction of Edward's apartments.

The cloth King Edward had sent home with me was quickly turned into a wedding gown by my mother's dressmakers. For a week I was measured and draped and prodded and turned and remarked upon. It was beautiful cloth and I should have been happy, but I wasn't. I was miserable with worry about Edward. He could, at any given moment, be dead, and we would never know it. So I went about my days knowing that while I ate, or studied, or was measured for that fool gown, Edward might be lying dead in the palace, and us none the wiser.

He didn't come to my wedding, of course. I could scarce say that I was at my own wedding, although I distinctly recollect parts of it.

It was on Whitsunday, which was the twenty-first of May, that I was wed. We took the barge on the river to Durham House in the Strand. It was one of Northumberland's great houses, and I remember how it was refurbished with Turkish carpets and new hangings of crimson and gold tissue, how we were received by the Northumberlands, the Warwicks, the Pembrokes, the Winchesters.

My gold-and-silver-brocaded gown was sewn with diamonds and pearls. My ladies braided pearls into my hair, which fell to my shoulders. And the whole Privy Council was present. I was aware of the closeness of my sister Catherine, for it was a double wedding. Of her echoing my saying of the vows, of the music, and all our attendants and my beaming parents. But it was like a dream. I was and was not there.

I was aware of Guildford standing beside me, resplendent in his best court clothes, his responses to the vows, but I felt nothing for him. I knew this should have been the happiest of days for me. But it was not. I was miserable.

Afterward there was feasting, masques, and jousting in the true royal manner. I kept looking for King Edward, hoping he might manage to come at the last moment. And all the while thinking of him as already dead.

I dreaded being alone with Guildford as wife to husband. But then the only good thing to happen that day happened.

It was decided by Northumberland, who was running the whole affair, that my sister and I should not yet live with our husbands.

"That way he can still have the marriages annulled if need be," Guildford Dudley said jokingly. Was he disappointed? I think not. No more than I was.

So I went to Chelsea Manor because it now belonged to Northumberland. Catherine went to Pembroke House.

∼SIXTEEN∼

So I was back again at Chelsea Manor, where I'd spent so many happy hours with Katharine and Sir Thomas and Elizabeth. Impossible to believe I was back here. I wandered about the place, touching things. Many of Katharine's possessions were still here, her books, her clothing, her bedhangings, even her pillows. I felt her presence all around me, eerie and ghostlike. Everything had her touch on it.

My nurse and Mrs. Tilney, as well as other members of my household, were with me, but my parents were not. I was weary beyond thinking and couldn't wait to get out of my wedding attire and go to bed. I slept in Katharine's bed, in her room. I drifted off as if I never had a care in the world, with Pourquoi at my feet.

To keep sane I stayed with my schedule. Up early, prayers, breakfast, studies, then in the afternoon my dancing lessons and some time for my music. I could ride if I wished. But still, I felt both the haunted and the ghost. Katharine's bedchamber was now mine, and I had to rearrange it in order to make it my own.

There were the same fish in the goldfish pond. Sir Thomas had named them and he used to feed them. And now they came to the surface. There was the rose arbor we'd all sat under on warm afternoons to watch the boats go by on the river.

There was the spot Katharine had caught Elizabeth in her husband's arms. There we'd run with the dogs and tossed a ball.

In my free time I wandered. I read. I embroidered. I became lonely for callers. I think I would have welcomed even Guildford, but he did not come. He was home with his mother.

And then one day, one of my ladies, Eleanor, who'd been to court to see her sister who was ill, came back with news.

"Northumberland says King Edward is walking in his galleries," she said. "That he is playing at quoits."

"Don't believe it," my nurse said. "I heard he is very ill."

"My sister says gossip has it that Northumberland has written to both Mary and Elizabeth, asking them to come to London, and they won't go," Eleanor reported.

"But why does he want them both in London?" I asked.

"Because Edward is dying is why," Mrs. Tilney advised. "He wouldn't ask them if Edward were well."

"Then why won't they go?" Eleanor tried to reason.

"Because they're afraid Northumberland will imprison them," she answered.

"And make whom Queen?" I asked.

"Mayhap no Queen. Mayhap he has plans to make one of his sons king," she jested. "Mayhap Guildford." And she laughed.

But I did not consider it a jest. Northumberland was capable of anything.

The days of that spring and early summer went on. I felt out of sorts at Chelsea Manor. I tried to concentrate on my studies, but my mind would not be put to the task.

And then one day a rider came up to the postern gate and dismounted. He had no servant, and he was not dressed in the glitter of the court.

He asked for me at the gate, and at first I thought he was just a messenger from home.

"I am John Banister," he introduced himself, "a student doctor attached to the royal household. All the doctors have been dismissed."

My heart fell. "Is the king dying, then?"

"Yes, he is dying." The young man was thin of face, and tall, and already looked like a doctor. I invited him to sit in my parlor and ordered some wine for him.

"I promised him I'd come to see you," Banister said. "I went first to Bradgate, but your father directed me here. He sends his best wishes."

"And Edward? What of Edward?" I begged. "What word does he have for me?"

He sipped his wine. "To be brave," he said.

"Brave? Why? Why must needs I be brave?"

He shook his head. "He doesn't sleep unless he is filled with drugs," he said quietly. "He brings up black sputum when he coughs. His feet are swollen."

I shivered.

"Northumberland sent us away and put a female quack in our place. She says she can cure him. And she gives him daily portions of a medicine that I know contains arsenic."

"Arsenic! That alone will kill him!"

He shook his head no. "In small doses, it is keeping him alive, though he be in pain."

"Why? Why make him suffer?"

"Northumberland needs time with him yet. He is buying time. When I bade him good-bye, Edward begged me to stop and see you and tell you he is bearing up and thinks of you often, and must make his will, and wishes you to know he has faith that you will do the right thing when the time comes."

"The right thing?" I was crying already. "What does he

want me to do? Did he say?"

"No, but when I left, he reminded me to tell you how sorry he is that he missed your wedding. And how sorry he is that he had to sign the death warrant for Edward Seymour. But that it is 'what kings must do.'"

Edward "sorry" because he missed my wedding! He was dying! Possibly being slowly poisoned, in pain, having to make his will at fifteen, and sorry he missed my wedding. Oh, Edward, the only dear true friend I had in the world.

The young doctor had to leave. He would not stay for a repast. The day was waning and he wanted to be in London this night. I bade him good-bye and watched from the gate as he rode away. The afternoon sun was strong, but I felt, for all the turmoil inside me, that it should be dark and forboding.

My next visitor was the Duchess of Northumberland, wife of Northumberland, and my mother-in-law.

This was an imperious woman, even more imperious than my own mother. I hoped never to have to go up against her. She came with a whole retinue of ladies-in-waiting and servants, and my household scurried about to make her comfortable. She demanded wine. She demanded we be left alone to talk.

The woman had given birth to thirteen children, seven of whom lived. It was said of Northumberland's household that his wife and children were affectionate and loyal.

How would anyone dare be anything else with such parents as the Duchess and Northumberland? I wondered.

"I have come to tell you, Lady Jane," she said imperiously, "if God should call the King to His mercy, it will be needful for you to go immediately to the Tower."

"Why?" I felt a chill.

"Because His Majesty has made you heir to his realm."

Heir? I couldn't believe it. When had this happened? How could this be? I followed her from the room. My head was spinning. The sun shone down outside. She smiled at me in satisfaction, as if to say, *See what wonders come about because you have wed my son?*

I did not believe her. Not for a minute. She was taunting me. She did not like me, this woman. Considered me not worthy of Guildford.

"Guildford, of course, must take himself there too," she added. And then: "He misses you. He pines for you, Jane. My darling boy."

I wondered what she was plotting. Anything for Guildford, of course. But how much power did they have? I shivered, not wishing to know the answer. But not for a minute did I believe her. I saw her out, wondering what her real motive had been for coming.

By July second we heard, from a friend of Mrs. Tilney's who'd been at court, that King Edward was begging God to take him.

We heard that Northumberland was preventing both Mary and Elizabeth from seeing their dying brother.

The summer quiet lay about Chelsea Manor, like the calm before a storm. Sometimes I went outside and walked along the riverbank just to hear the sound of the gulls flying overhead. Their cry echoed something lost and wandering in my soul.

I felt as if the world were standing still, as if this were my last chance to look around and enjoy it before plunging into an abyss. I felt like a prisoner here, and yet I knew I was safe. I thought of all the good people I'd known. I wondered what Queen Katharine and Sir Thomas would have to say about all that was happening.

Northumberland was in charge, running the kingdom. I had the feeling he was moving people around on a chessboard. I could see him, grinning, leaning over it.

On the eighth of July rumor ran through the countryside that Edward VI had died.

Our milkmaids had it before we did. Rumor travels swiftly, faster than sound, faster than the wind and the tides.

I knew it this time not to be rumor, though. When the common people had such intelligence, you could be sure it was true. I waited for something to happen. And very soon it did.

SEVENTEEN

The first I knew that something was truly amiss was when a rider came through the countryside crying the fact that Princess Mary was gone. That she had retreated to Norfolk, dressed as a boy, to board a ship and flee the country.

The rider was not from Northumberland or the palace. He wore nobody's colors. He just had news and was spreading it for his own ends, accepting coins of the realm, and meat and drink, for his trouble and enjoying himself immeasurably.

Sometimes when ordinary folk got hold of rumor they did this. Carried it through the countryside. People were hungry for news.

"She stayed the night at Sawson Hall near Cambridge,"

the man told us. "It's the manor house of John Huddlestone, a Catholic gentleman. He received her gladly, 'tis said, had mass said in his house for her. In the morning after they rode off, some Protestants in Cambridge set fire to the house, thinking she was still inside. It is said that Mary saw it from a hilltop and told John Huddlestone that when she was Queen she would build him an even better house."

"Why is she fleeing if she hopes to be Queen?" Mrs. Tilney asked. We stood in the courtyard, in the sun.

"It is said that Northumberland ordered three important Catholic prisoners in the Tower to be executed this day, lest they take up the banner and support Mary."

"But she is supposed to be Queen," I put in.

The messenger shrugged and gulped his brew, seeing that we were growing impatient with him. "I must be off. It is all the news I have this day. Perhaps I'll be back tomorrow."

The next day he did come back. Mrs. Tilney sent me out alone, not wishing to be subject, as she said to "more lies."

"A fleet of seven great warships now wait off the eastern coast, in the event that Mary tries to flee the country," he told us. "Northumberland cannot have her bringing in supporters from another country to help her with her pretensions to the crown."

"But she is not pretending," I said.

A number of servants who had gathered around nodded in agreement with me.

"Northumberland has informed Princess Elizabeth of her brother's death."

I wondered how Elizabeth was feeling.

"Princess Mary slept last night at Euston Hall, near Thetford, the home of a friend. She now travels disguised as a serving maid. A courier of Northumberland's intercepted her and told her that she cannot hope to prevail against Northumberland. That she cannot escape from England because the way is barred by warships on the eastern coast."

I knew Mary well enough to reason that, told such, she would only press on harder to her goal.

Northumberland did not know her. He only thought he did.

The next day I had another caller: Lady Mary Sydney, daughter of Northumberland. She came by way of the river, with a retinue of ladies.

"It is necessary that you come with me immediately," she said when I had received her. "We must go on to Syon House, my father's mansion at Isleworth on the Thames."

"Why?" I inquired.

"Don't ask, just do as you are told," my mother said. Then she ordered one of my ladies to pack some of my things. I should have been suspicious of something, because my best dresses were packed with care. And in a short time I found myself on Lady Mary's barge along with Mother and Mrs. Tilney, to take the water to Syon House.

Mother would not tell us why we were being taken there. And we did not press her to know. But she had a pleased smile on her face that made me suspect they were all in congress about something.

The sun was hot on the water, in spite of the silk canopy over us. A musician on board played the lute skillfully. We passed the gilded barge of the Lord Mayor and he waved at us. Seagulls swooped and cried overhead, following us, as if to say, "Beware, Lady Jane, beware."

I tried to keep from being frightened. I was Protestant, so I knew I was safe, but all kinds of people were being moved about on Northumberland's chessboard since Edward's death.

On the shore, farmers and their helpers came to the water's edge, waving at us, knowing we were somehow connected to royalty. The girls threw flowers into the water. I waved back.

When we arrived at the water gate for Syon House, we were greeted respectfully by Northumberland's servants. They helped us out of the barge, Mother first. And we made our way up the steps and into the great hall of the house.

At first it seemed deserted except for a few stray servants who brought us wine and sweetmeats.

"It is requested that all of you wait here, madam," one of the servants said. And she left us.

I looked around at the Persian carpets, the magnificent tapestries.

"This used to be a convent," Lady Mary told me.

Yes, I thought. *One of the many seized by Henry VIII and now by Northumberland.*

Soon we heard footsteps echoing on the marble hall floors, and Northumberland, my father, and the whole of the Privy Council came into the room to join us. Hellos were said but the Council and Northumberland stood a way apart, discussing something in low voices. Then my husband, Guildford Dudley, came running into the room, late and apologizing.

His father gestured to him, and he came to my side and bowed. "Good morrow, Lady Jane."

"Good morrow," I said.

He stood to one side of me, my mother to the other, waiting. It seemed like everyone was waiting and everyone but me knew what they were waiting for.

Northumberland gave the faintest of signals with his head and then two of the Council, Pembroke and Huntingdon, came over to speak to me. I raised my head to listen.

But they did not speak.

They knelt. They called me their sovereign lady. I

thought they were mad to give me such honor. I looked at my mother and she shrugged. I looked at Guildford and he smiled.

Northumberland and the rest of the council were smiling too.

"Is there something you are not telling me, my lords?" I asked. "Why do you do me this semblance of honor? I am not your sovereign lady."

"Ah, but you are, Lady Jane." Northumberland stepped forward a pace or two.

He paused and said something to one of the council, who immediately left the room. Then he proceeded to approach me and extended his arm. "Come with me, Lady Jane. Do not be fearful, child."

But I was fearful. Northumberland was up to some terrible mischief. I knew that. And he had made me part of it. I took his arm and we all walked slowly into another great room even more lavishly decorated.

In the middle of the room was a chair with a rich canopy over it. He led me to the chair. My mother-in-law was waiting in this room and a number of other noble persons. As Northumberland led me to the chair, they started to bow and curtsey to me.

I stopped. "Wait. You must tell me what this is all about," I begged. "Why is everyone doing me such reverence?"

Northumberland gave a great sigh and commenced to

speak as if he'd been waiting a long time for this. "As President of the Council I do now declare the death of his most blessed and gracious Majesty, King Edward VI. He shall be sorely missed."

Murmurs of assent from all in the room.

Northumberland continued. I don't recollect half he said. It was all about defending the kingdom from the popish faith and the rule of the King's evil sisters. It was about my mother, graciously waiving her right to the throne. And then:

"His Majesty hath named your grace as heir to the crown of England. Your sisters will succeed you in the case of your default of issue."

The floor moved beneath my feet. My head felt light. The numerous candles hurt my eyes. Peoples' faces wavered in front of me.

Northumberland was still going on. About God now, and how He was the sovereign and disposer of all crowns and scepters, and how He had advanced me.

Then, of a sudden, all in the room knelt before me. Even my mother and father who had slapped and scolded me so.

Northumberland assured me that each one in the room would shed blood for me. Gladly.

It was then that I fainted.

~EIGHTEEN~

Nobody approached me as I lay on the floor in a faint. I became conscious soon enough, but still lay there, with no strength to rise.

My mother's voice came to me through a mist in front of my eyes and what seemed like a hood over my ears. "Get up, Jane. We raised you better than that."

If I was Queen, how could she scold me, was my only thought. Tears came to my eyes then. *Why were these people tormenting me?* was all I could think. I had done everything they wanted, hadn't I?

Then Guildford knelt over me. He was all dressed in white, gold, and silver. "Jane. Wife. Get up. You are Queen now. Your subjects await you."

He helped me to my feet. The only reason I let him was

because I was starting to feel silly prone on the floor with everybody staring at me. I stood and shook off Guildford's hand on my arm.

"God save you, Jane Grey," Northumberland said. "God save the Queen."

They'd all gotten to their feet and were staring at me. "I am not the Queen," I said in a tremulous voice. "I am only a girl of fifteen."

"Edward was fifteen and just coming into his majority when he died," Northumberland reminded me.

"The crown is not my right. I don't want it. Princess Mary is the rightful heir."

Anger set Northumberland's face in hard lines. He was not accustomed to being argued with. "Your Grace does wrong to herself and to her house!"

Then he turned to my parents. "You said the girl was brought up to this. You said she would be amenable."

"Jane Grey"—my mother spoke sharply—"do not disgrace yourself, your family, your father and your mother. We have brought you up to be an obedient daughter. And anyway, the matter of your inheriting the crown was in Edward's will! He wanted you as Queen. Do you deny him?"

I said nothing. "Be brave" was the message he had sent me with Dr. Banister.

"You professed your love for him while he lived, and now you denounce his wishes, when he is not here to defend them?"

My father spoke. But softly, as he always did. "Jane, think what will happen if Mary takes the throne. She is Catholic. She must soon, as Queen, wed. She will no doubt pick a Spanish prince. The Spanish have been conducting a most dolorous Inquisition, killing all who are not of their faith. We will have an Inquisition in England, and all of us will die if Mary is named Queen. It is your duty, child."

"What about Elizabeth?" I asked.

"You know those who would make Mary Queen believe that Elizabeth is illegitimate," my father said soothingly. "You learned this at your mother's knee."

They made sense, but I could not be sure. I needed time.

"And, as daughter of a princess, your mother has waived her right to the throne so it may go to you," my father added, making me feel twice as guilty.

"I have to pray," I said. It was the only way to get time.

All nodded and agreed, and I knelt down on the floor right there and bowed my head. But I could not pray. All I could do was try to stop my head from spinning.

Jane Grey, Queen of England!

I had freckles. I had sandy hair. I was too short. Would my feet even touch the floor if I sat on the throne? What would I do as ruler? What did queens do all day long? I knew that kings went hunting, pursued women, played at cards, jousted in tornaments, and signed death warrants.

Kings also roared when angry, ate great amounts of

food, ordered court entertainments. How could I do all those things?

Who would listen to a woman, much less a short, freckle-faced girl? What did I know of matters of state, the doings of the Privy Council, foreign ambassadors?

These people were all addled in the head.

But what would happen if I refused?

Elizabeth would reign. And Mary would try to dispose of her, and they would end up killing each other. Then I'd have to be Queen anyway. And I'd have two dead princesses on my conscience.

But what would keep Mary from trying to dispose of me? She could put spies in my court. I could be poisoned. They could loosen the cinch of my saddle when I rode, and I could fall and break my neck.

I shivered and looked at Northumberland, who was eyeing me darkly. "Who will protect me if Mary decides to do away with me?" I asked.

"You heard, Jane. All of us are willing to spill blood for you."

"I will protect you." Guildford squatted down next to me.

Well, that counted for nothing. All he wanted was to be King. That was why Northumberland had had us wed. He'd been planning this all along.

"I know nothing about matters of state," I told Northumberland.

"Your Privy Council runs things."

I sighed. I felt like a dog in a bear-baiting contest, running around with no way out. There was no way out. I knew that now. Well, I might as well act graciously and not disgrace my family. Besides, mother would whip me if I did.

"May I still study as I wish?" I asked Northumberland.

"You may study to your heart's content, Lady Jane. And let us worry how to run the kingdom."

That was what he wanted of course, to run the kingdom. Well, what could I do about it, I, just a girl? If I refused, he might maneuver to make his son Guildford King, and I didn't want that. I sighed deeply. If the country was going to hell, I might as well be on the throne as anyone else. I could keep some fairness alive.

"Think," my mother said, "think of all the Protestants who will not be burned at the stake because you are on the throne. Think of how they will be destroyed if Mary takes over."

For once in my life, she was right. I stood up from my prayers and faced them. "If what has been given to me is lawfully mine, may Divine Majesty help me to govern with spirit and grace and to the advantage of the realm," I said.

I managed to say it without a quiver in my voice too. They all clapped. And they seated me on the makeshift throne under the canopy.

NINETEEN

We had to make a grand entrance into London the next day, so everybody could see me as Queen. All around me people were in a state of frenzy, assembling clothing for me to wear. I must wear the Tudor colors, white and green. I must have a green damask kirtle. I must have a gem-encrusted French hood.

Mother insisted on three-inch-high chopines, which are wooden platform shoes, because I was too short and would not be seen in a procession. They must be found immediately.

Guildford would wear white, gold, and silver, walk beside me, and bow low to me each time I spoke with him. It was almost worth all the insanity, just to have Guildford bow low to me.

Mother would be my train bearer. Mother would carry my train, she who had slapped me and beaten me and pinched me.

There was some good in all this, then. There was justice in the world!

Six noblemen would carry the canopy of state over my head as we headed for the Tower, where all kings and queens went to stay in the royal apartments before they were crowned.

I was never alone now. My sisters fluttered around me. Little Mary kept saying "Queen Jane, Queen Jane." It was worth it to see her so happy.

But we were not to have a procession in the streets. We were to travel on the royal barge on the Thames. A flotilla of other barges would go before us, filled with those of the Privy Council and important members of state.

I shivered, seeing all the fuss. I was hot one minute and cold the next. I was hungry, and I couldn't eat a morsel when it was brought to me. Mother rubbed my hands, taking them in her own, as she had never before done.

My father kept saying encouraging things to me. Every minute one of my ladies inquired as to whether I had need of something. They combed my hair. They perfumed it. They plaited it with pearls and flowers. I sneezed and they said, "God save the Queen."

God save me. I couldn't save myself!

People of my household told me there was "a strong military presence in the city," the next morning when I took breakfast. Northumberland had arranged it. He stood before me.

"We have the royal heralds out announcing that you are Queen. I have reports they have already made the announcement in Cheapside and are continuing on through the city."

He did not look happy.

"What is the response of the people?" I asked.

"The trumpeters are blowing fanfares. There are shouts of 'God Save the Queen' from many sources."

That told me all I needed to know. "The people are not happy," I stated flatly.

"They will be," Northumberland insisted. "Only one man, who works at an inn, said Princess Mary should be Queen in your stead. We have taken him in hand."

"What have you done with him?" I asked.

"We have had his ears cut off."

"I want no one's ears cut off on my account." I faced Northumberland, and he glared at me. My gaze was cold and hard.

He smiled and gave a little bow. "No more ear cutting," he agreed. Why did I have the feeling he was only assuaging me?

"At midday the royal heralds will make the announcement at the Tower, at St. Paul's Cathedral, and in

Westminster. And again at Cheapside this evening."

"I want no more maiming of my people," I insisted.

Northumberland gave a bow. Was he mocking me? "Yes, Your Majesty," he said.

It was a pleasant summer's day when we took the royal barge to the Tower. It was decorated with the royal canopy and there were musicians on board. The water was calm, and people lined the shore on both sides of the river, but there was no cheering as we went by. A few little girls threw flowers into the water, but that was all.

"The people don't want me," I said to my mother.

"If they don't, they are fools," she said quietly. "Mary would burn them at the stake for not being Catholic."

She was so sure of this that it frightened me. I gave a little whimper of fear, and Mrs. Tilney patted my head. My ladies-in-waiting smiled at me in encouragement. More and more people were gathering on the shore as we reached the Tower. What if they rioted?

I looked for Northumberland, but he was in one of the barges up ahead.

"What if they riot?" I asked Guildford, who sat next to me in the barge.

"They wouldn't dare," he answered. "My father would have them driven into the Thames."

He was so sure of himself. He was having a good time, waving at the people on the shore. He had the other arm around me possessively, and though I did not love him, I could not shake him off—it would not look right. So I smiled instead, and was carried to the Tower, all on that summer's day.

There was great fanfare as we came to the water gate of the Tower. Yeomen of the guard stood around, barring anyone from getting near me. Northumberland helped me, then my mother, up the stone steps. There was a booming salute from the guns on the Tower wharf. It echoed off the water and through my bones. I did not like guns. Then Northumberland assembled the procession, again with Mother carrying my train.

There was the canopy of state, over me again. There were the trumpets. There were the people staring as we passed by on our way to the royal apartments.

"Why, she's just a child," I heard one woman remark as I clomped by on my wooden shoes. "A mere child."

"So was King Edward," someone reminded her.

Oh, Edward!

"Hold your head up," came the savage whisper from behind me. Mother. She might carry my train, but it was my guess that she would still slap me in private.

I held my head up. Tears rolled quietly down my face.

Waiting to meet us at the royal apartments were the Marquess of Winchester, my sister Catherine and her husband, Lieutenant of the Tower Sir John Bridges, and more yeomen of the guard. Sir Winchester went on his knees.

It made me uncomfortable to have anyone on his knees in front of me. I whispered this to my mother and she reached forward and pinched the back of my arm.

"Well, you'd better get used to it," she whispered.

Winchester made a pretty speech, and then offered me the great keys of the Tower, but Northumberland reached out and took them instead.

We went into the White Tower, and here were more people waiting to receive me. And here they had a throne and I had to sit on it.

Northumberland went down on his knees. "Welcome, Your Majesty," he said, "and as soon as it pleases you, we are having divine services in the Norman Chapel of St. John up in the keep."

"It pleases me," I said.

～TWENTY～

They brought the crown jewels to me that fine summer's day. The crown itself rested on a red velvet pillow with gold tassels and was brought by one of the elder Northumberland's men.

"Try it, milady," he insisted.

Mother stepped forward to smooth my hair. It was she who took the crown and set it on my head.

I had all I could do to hold my head up, it was so heavy. Edward had really worn this?

"I can't," I said. "I won't."

Mother slapped my arm and took the crown off. "Silly child. Won't wear the crown. How did we bring you up? You'll wear it when need be."

"I'm not a silly child," I lashed back. "I'm Queen."

"Then behave as such. And wear it."

But I wouldn't. And I remembered my own promise to myself to throw the crown at them if they ever made me wear it. Guildford was seated next to me on the throne. He put his arm around me. "Don't fret, Jane. I'll wear one with you," he whispered.

"What?"

But his mother had heard him. "He said he'd wear one with you. We're having another made for him."

There was something amiss here, but I put the thought in the back of my mind to be dealt with later. They were bringing the rest of the crown jewels to me, boxes of them for my inspection. I must open the boxes and admire them.

That evening there was a great banquet in the Tower with everyone present. The food was good and the company cheerful to the point of being riotous. I never remembered seeing my parents so happy. Mother was drinking a lot of wine and remembering her own girlhood. Father was looking on her with outright love.

Then he gave a toast, "To the woman who raised a queen!" And everyone cheered.

Guildford's parents were deep in conversation with mine. Guildford sat next to me, whispering loving things into my ear. And every so often he would say, "When we rule, Jane, when we rule—"

I must stop this immediately, I thought. *Tonight.* Could

anyone imagine Guildford ruling England?

My thoughts, and indeed the whole banquet, were interrupted then by the arrival of a man announced as Thomas Hungate.

"A messenger from Princess Mary," the yeoman of the guard announced him.

Everyone fell silent. The man came in walking proudly and stood there with a letter in his hand. Northumberland reached for it, and we all waited while he read it.

He remained stone-faced, then bade the servants give the man some food and drink, and he was ushered outside.

"She has evaded all capture," Northumberland said of Mary. "She intends to advance her claim to the throne."

A murmur of concern went around the banquet table. Northumberland held up his hand. "Don't worry, any of you. She is a woman alone. She has no resources. And I think her quite mad. She writes"—and he laughed and read a part of the letter—"'The other night in the storm I saw my father, Henry VIII, on the battlements of Whitehall. It has been reported to me that he was seen at Windsor and Hampton Court also, standing on the battlements and shouting into the storm. And he is angry.'

"Her mind has gone," Northumberland insisted. "She is seeing things."

He did not say anything about the other people who had seen the ghost of Henry VIII, raving into the storm, however. We went back to eating. But the banquet was noticeably quieter and there were no more toasts.

That evening Guildford came into my bedchamber, but I was determined that he should not stay. I was determined that he should not touch me. Ever. I had not wanted him as a husband and I would not have to do with him.

"Jane, my love"—and he reached for me—"what say you about the crown for me?"

I backed away. "Never," I told him.

"What?"

"Never."

"But I must be crowned King so I can sit beside you and help you rule."

"You couldn't rule a court jester, Guildford. Now be sensible. I can have you made a duke, but only Parliament can make you King, and I don't hear anything about them setting out to do it. Do you?"

"But you are Queen. And you rule."

He was handsome, all right, although if I had to marry one of the Dudleys, I would have preferred his younger brother, Robert. Not as handsome, Robert was noble when you saw him in action. Guildford was never driven to action. He was handsome, round faced and childish, and when he didn't get his own way and his lip curled under, he was ugly.

"I rule, yes," I said, "and I choose to make you a duke. Not King."

He stamped his foot like a girl. "I'll not stand for it," he said, pouting.

"You'll have to, I'm afraid. Now leave me. I want no sulking in my bedchamber. I want no whining child."

"I am your husband!"

"For convenience only. Leave me, please."

He turned and slammed out. As he went, I heard him calling, "Mother, Mother, do you hear this? Mother? I need you."

She came back in with him in minutes. She was a large woman, massive about the shoulders, and I think she disliked me because I was small. "What is this I hear, daughter-in-law? My son is distressed."

"He wants to be made King and I have refused him."

"And what right have you to do so? He is your husband."

"It is nothing I sought, or wanted. He can be my husband, but he will not be King. Only Parliament can make him King, and they are not about to do so."

"You can insist on it."

"But I will not. The crown is not a toy. I don't even want it myself. And I won't bestow it on him."

"Well, of all the insolence! Wait until your mother hears about this."

"I am Queen," I told her. "And I will not suffer either

one of you to question my decisions."

"Come, Guildford"—and she took his hand—"you don't want to be husband to an ungrateful little baggage like this. You will not bed her. I will not allow it."

I sighed with relief and thought, *Thank you, mother-in-law. Thank you.*

Of course, the celebrations did not go on forever. There was routine. Anybody who thinks a queen sits around all day eating sweetmeats and ordering people around should have another thought. There was a whole new course of study now, which I set to eagerly. I remembered how much studying Edward had to do as King, and I thought again, *Oh, Edward!*

The Privy Council met mornings, but I did not go. What would I do at a Privy Council meeting? Guildford went, and I let him go to quiet him. His father made all the decisions anyway.

I was paid a visit by Sir John Cheke on the following morning as I set myself to my books. He was an elderly, kind man, with long thin hands and a gentle manner. He had once been Edward's tutor and was learned in the ways of our religion.

"I would fain help you with your studies," he said, "if you are not ahead of me. I hear you are an excellent scholar."

I wanted to hug the man. Edward had loved him. And

think of the remembrances he could tell me about my cousin! "Oh sir, you are too kind. Come in, come in, and sit. I shall send for some wine for you. Oh, I would be honored to have you as tutor! And you knew Edward well, then?"

He chuckled quietly. "No one knew him better."

"Oh sir, sit, do."

Northumberland sent letters for me to sign. They were to foreign ambassadors. So many letters. I read them over, just to be sure I wasn't signing someone's death warrant. You could never tell with Northumberland. But I did not understand the letters. And when I wailed once to Sir Cheke that I never hoped to understand matters of state, he told me not to worry, that Northumberland wouldn't let me make such decisions anyway. But I should ask him any question I wanted, and perhaps he could at least explain things to me.

The noon dinner lasted for two hours and was very formal. I must sit between my mother and mother-in-law, with all the members of the council and all the lords at the table. But I listened to everything being said. And I learned that Londoners were not happy with my being Queen. I learned that one of the privy councillors, William Cecil, was working to restore Mary to the throne. I learned that Mary was still wandering around out there somewhere. That Robert Dudley was trying to capture her.

I learned that Princess Elizabeth was ill, or pretending to be ill.

I signed everything Northumberland gave me to sign. I signed "Jane the Queen." Sometimes he explained the papers to me and sometimes he didn't.

I learned that in Norfolk and Suffolk, in Berkshire and Buckinghamshire, in Gloucestershire and Oxfordshire, men were arming and giving their loyal support to Mary as Queen.

Would Mary forgive me for taking the throne if she came into power? Or would she have me taken prisoner? We had always been friends in the past. I knew her to be a kind and forgiving person.

But the throne. It wasn't like taking a morsel off someone's plate.

I became ill then. I lost my appetite and could not eat. I could swear that my hair was falling out. The skin on my hands started to peel. I knew that Northumberland had been whispered about in connection with poisoning King Edward when he was ill, and I grew fearful that he was poisoning me.

He was poisoning me because I would not make his son Guildford King.

I lay in my bed alone and cried. Then I heard that Northumberland had left the Tower to muster some troops at Tothill Fields near Westminster, to go against Mary, who was at Kenninghall. And I thought, *There will be war and people will be killed for me. To defend my right to wear the crown, which I don't even want.*

I wanted to forget it all and go home. I wanted to go to Chelsea Manor and study my Greek and Latin and forget matters of state. I wanted to be what I was: a fifteen-year-old girl.

I was lying on my bed one day when my mother came to my chambers. "Jane, get up. Northumberland is ready to ride out, and you must have a good word for him."

"I'm not well."

"You are Queen, Jane. You cannot give in to the weaknesses of ordinary people. Get up and put on your new blue dress and silver kirtle. Now."

"My hair is falling out."

"Your hair is not falling out, Jane. Don't look for excuses. Northumberland is about to go and fight for your crown. The least you could do is give him a good word before he leaves."

I did so, although my legs were weak and my hands were sweating. My ladies-in-waiting helped me to get ready, and I went downstairs into the receiving hall and waited for Northumberland.

I heard him and his men come into the courtyard outside with a great clatter and neighing of horses. Then the large doors swung open and he came in.

He was dressed in armor and looked very knightly, and he had with him all his sons except Guildford. The Privy

Council gathered around.

"Mary has fourteen thousand men," he said. "We have five thousand. We ride now to defend Your Majesty and know God to be on our side. I caution all who ride with me that your estates and families are in our hands."

For the first time I was taken with Northumberland, who was ready to ride out to defend my right to the throne. He ran things, yes. He made decisions, but he was willing to lay his life down for that right. And for me.

"I pray you, use your diligence," I told him.

He bowed. "I will do what in me lies," he said.

And in the next moment they were gone.

~TWENTY-ONE~

Everyone in the Tower with me—my mother-in-law, my nurse and ladies-in-waiting, the Privy Council and even Guildford—tried to make things as normal as possible, but I sensed an undercurrent of activity all around me.

The Privy Council was meeting in secret behind closed doors. With Northumberland gone, this was not good. I know he feared their betrayal. What were they meeting about? I supposed as Queen I could break in on the meeting, but I would not know what to do when I got there, so I stayed away.

The next day reports began coming from Northumberland.

He'd been defeated in a fight at Cambridge. His men

were deserting and going over to Mary. But worse yet, the fleet of ships in the harbor had all declared for Mary.

My father came to visit me. "Some members of the Privy Council are defecting," he said.

"Why?"

"Mary grows stronger by the day, Jane. But Northumberland is recruiting the peasants from the countryside to fight for you. You are not to worry. Everything will be fine. Mary will soon be captured."

"I don't want her hurt," I said.

Guildford, who was with my father, sneered. "You worry about her? She'd have us both clapped in irons in a minute. Worry about us."

"I'm sure you're doing enough of that for both of us, Guildford."

"Stop this, both of you," my father ordered. "Don't you think, with all that's going on, that you two could call a truce?" Then he left us.

Guildford and I looked at each other, shamefaced. "He's right," Guildford said. "Mary has been proclaimed Queen at both Oxford and Norwich. He didn't want to tell you. I think your throne is in danger, Jane."

"I'd be happy as a child with sweetmeats if she'd take it," I said.

"You don't know what you're saying!" He leaned forward, angry. "This is a kingdom we're talking about here. My father is out fighting for you. The least you could do is care."

"I do care."

"Then act it. People look to you."

I started to cry then. "Oh, Guildford, I don't want them looking to me. Don't you understand?"

He sat down beside me then and took my hands in his. He said absolutely nothing, and as far as I was concerned it was the most tender he ever acted with me. And I started to forgive him, just a little bit.

Lady Eleanor, one of my ladies-in-waiting, came to me. "Your Highness, I beg leave to go out of this place and return home. My mother is ill and needs me."

She was the second one this day. The first had been Lady Dorothy.

I was not fooled. "You wish to declare for Mary?"

"No, no." She bowed even lower. "My mother truly is ill. Oh, I will stay if you wish it, but I fear for her."

"Go," I said. "I pray your mother gets well soon. When she does, come back to me."

"Yes, Your Highness."

But I knew I would never see her again.

I thought a lot about Mary in the next couple of days. How did it feel to want the throne so badly that you were willing to roam the countryside and evade capture for it? How did it feel to have all the towns and shires, even the ships in the harbor, declaring for you?

What would she do when she got it? I was nobody's fool, no matter what they thought of me. I knew she would win. She was truly a princess of the blood. Her father had ... ing. Had she really seen him on the battlements? ... veling around in been a k~~ing~~

I tried to picture her in my mind, ~~tra~~ ~~~~~ ~~~~~
disguise, fighting for her life. I knew her to be pale and
homely, but I also knew she had strengths I did not. And
the people wanted her.

Two days later word came to us. Mary was proclaimed
Queen in London. Northumberland had torn down a banner proclaiming me Queen. But of course he would. To
stand for me when she was hailed Queen was to ask for
death for treason. What could I do for him and his now?

When I ventured out of my chambers I found the
Tower quiet as a tomb. Where was everybody? A page
told me all in the Privy Council had left. And that
Northumberland had been arrested for treason.

I was at the noon meal with Mrs. Tilney and Guildford
when my father came into the banquet hall. He came right
to me and stood there, white faced and grim.

Then, in one sweeping movement he tore the canopy
of state down from over my head. "You are no longer
Queen," he said. "They are bringing Northumberland
back to be a prisoner in the Tower. You are finished."

"Can I go home now?" I asked.

He strode from the room without answering.

TWENTY-TWO

Nine days a queen, and I hated it.

What was to become of me now? I had a husband I near despised, a mother-in-law who hated me, and a father-in-law who was a prisoner in the Tower. My ladies, with the exception of Mrs. Tilney, had deserted me and proclaimed Mary Queen.

Then the worst came. I found out that my father and Sir Cheke had left the Tower too, to declare for Mary. Would people stop at nothing to save their own skins?

In the streets of London, I heard, the people were crying, "Long live Queen Mary!" and building bonfires all over, and ringing church bells.

They wanted Mary, the Catholic queen! Well, let them have her.

Mrs. Tilney did nothing but cry and walk around me wringing her hands, so that I had to order her from my presence, in order to think.

What would Mary do to me? I had no doubts that I'd be moved to the prisoners' part of the Tower. I expected to be put in a dungeon and mayhap chained to the wall.

Guildford burst in on me. "Jane, what is to happen to us?" He was in despair, his handsome face all twisted with pain. He was pacing, pulling at his hair, wishing for his mother.

"She's gone to Mary to plead Father's case," he said. "Why did she go when I need her now?"

"You don't need her, Guildford," I told him. "You have yourself."

"And you, Jane? Do I have you?"

"Yes, Guildford, but likely we will be kept apart. They will imprison us separately. You must remember to be dignified and not let them know you are afraid. It's all you have, isn't it?"

"It isn't much," he said. And I was inclined to agree with him.

True to my speculation, they moved us at the end of that day. Finally Mrs. Tilney packed my things. Then we were moved to the prisoners' part of the Tower. I was so afraid, I was trembling, but I could not let the others know it.

It was dark when we were moved, and we walked across

the Tower grounds to the accompaniment of torches and shadows and muted voices. I heard rushing water but could not see much beyond the rim of torchlight. We were going toward a half-timbered house, through a door, and up some steps, and then the torches were set in the walls.

It was not a dungeon, no, but the house of Master Partridge, gentleman jailor of the Tower. He welcomed me with a small bow.

"My lady," he said, "this overlooks Tower Green. Next door is Beauchamp Tower, where all the Dudleys are imprisoned. I am sorry. You are not allowed to see your husband."

"It's all right," I said.

I had a small room with a bed, a table, and some chairs. Clean and bare. I liked it.

"I shall see about getting you writing materials and books. And Queen Mary has said that you are to be treated kindly."

I liked that even better.

Mrs. Ellen had been my nurse since I was born. She was round faced and always wore blue and white. Ever since I could remember, those were the only colors she adorned herself in.

I didn't cry until we were left alone by the jailor and then for some reason I burst into tears. Mrs. Ellen held me and said, "There, there, it will be all right. You were always friends with Mary. She won't harm you."

It made sense of a sudden. Of course she was right. Mary and I had been friends ever since I could remember. The four of us had played together as children—Mary, Elizabeth, Edward, and I. How could Mary hurt me now?

Mrs. Ellen set about straightening my room while she told me the news she'd acquired when she stopped to talk to a guard on the way to our new abode.

Before he was arrested, Northumberland had thrown a hatful of gold coins into the crowd, then wept as he declared for Queen Mary.

The Earl of Pembroke had put my sister Catherine out of his house and declared her no longer wed to his son, since Northumberland's arrest.

"And your cousin Edward isn't buried yet. My Lord! Wouldn't you think they'd bury the lad and give him some rest?"

"Mary will," I said quickly. "She'll do it first thing. I know Mary."

"Mary," Nurse Ellen reported, "is wearing purple velvet and satin, in the French style. Her horse is caparisoned in gold cloth. I saw her when she rode into London. Everyone cheered. Elizabeth was by her side. And they tell the story that Elizabeth rode out to meet her on the road to London. And when she encountered her, Elizabeth got off her horse and knelt in the dust of the road before her sister."

The next day a man named Stephen Gardiner came to see me. He was tall and broad, and I'd known him once as one of Queen Katharine's enemies. He was now Mary's chief minister. And he made no bones about what he wanted.

"The crown jewels," he said to me.

"I don't have them."

"Nobody does. They are missing."

"Why ask me? I didn't take them."

"Say what you will. I've been to see your husband and gone through his things. I've taken every one of the jewels he had in his possession. And the money and expensive clothing he had."

I understood then. The crown jewels were not missing. But he was here to confiscate whatever I had that was worth anything, for his own use.

"I cannot stop you," I said. "Just leave me the clothes on my back."

Mrs. Ellen berated him, but to no end. He went through all my belongings. He took my two good necklaces that had been left to me, a purse of gold coins, and my best gowns and hoods that were sewn with pearls.

I slammed the door on him when he left. He would be the richer for his visit to me, but I cared not. What use had I for the jewels?

Mrs. Ellen told me the story of Princess Elizabeth when she was a toddler. "She'd been sent to live with Kat Ashley.

Her mother was executed when she was three, and after that she was no longer treated like a princess, but just a person of royal blood. Her clothes were so poor. Kat had to make her dresses and constantly write to her father to beg for fabric for the poor child," she related.

"Well, I'm not a child. I know I'm not considered a queen anymore and must take what I can get," I told her.

She would sew me some dresses, she reassured me, since Stephen Gardiner had taken all but the one I had on my back.

Master Partridge, gentleman jailor, and his wife became our friends. He was a quiet, rotund man, who seemed apologetic about everything.

Every evening we were invited to sit and take supper with them. It was a dignified, civilized affair, and I shall never forget Master Partridge's kindness to me.

We dined as a family—he and his wife, Alice, Mrs. Ellen, and myself. He smuggled books in to me, and his wife got some cloth for my dresses.

The talk alone was richer than the food. One night he told us how Northumberland had collapsed upon being brought to the Tower and told he would soon meet his death.

Another night he spoke of Queen Mary in whispered reverence. "She must soon wed," he told us. "And produce an heir, so Elizabeth and you can never become Queen. Once she has an heir, you will likely be released, Jane. Her kingdom will be safe."

"But whom will she wed?" I asked.

"Ah, whom?" And he rolled his eyes. "There are two in question. One Edward Courtney, who has been imprisoned in this very Tower for fifteen of his twenty-seven years."

"And all because he has royal blood and was a threat to the Tudor dynasty," his wife added.

The torchlight on the walls flickered as they told me of Edward Courtney, whom Queen Mary had released from the Tower. "We know him well," said Master Partridge. "For fifteen years of imprisonment he studied and learned several languages. He is a musician and artist, but the poor lad cannot even ride a horse."

"And who is the other she might wed, then?"

"Prince Philip the Second of Spain."

"Spain?" I shuddered. "No, no, not Spain. All of England will be under Spanish rule and religion."

"That is what many say, yes. And many fear," he agreed. "But the money is on Prince Philip of Spain."

"And when she weds and has an heir—" I started to say.

"You will be free, Jane," Master Partridge insisted. "So keep hope."

"Let us pray it won't take fifteen years," I said.

~TWENTY-THREE~

I suppose I could have endured years in prison, like Edward Courtney. But then he was the great-grandson of Edward IV, which was why he'd been imprisoned so long. I thought about Edward Courtney often in the days that followed, as the summer waned. I studied and played my music. I was allowed to have my dog, Pourquoi, but still I knew I could never abide fifteen years in this place.

I missed riding a horse, for one thing, though I had never been a good horsewoman. I missed it simply because I couldn't do it, as I missed being in the middle of people. I missed going outdoors. I was allowed out only at certain times to walk in the garden. My movements, no matter how kindly Master Partridge, were timed and watched.

At the same time I missed being alone. I was never alone. Mrs. Ellen was always with me, chatting cheerfully, telling stories or humming songs.

One day Master Partridge came to see me and handed me a note. It was from Guildford. I was sitting by the window, reading, and he waited while I read it.

Guildford wanted to meet with me. "It isn't allowed," I said, looking up into Master Partridge's placid face.

"Well now, Lady Jane, if you two were out walking at the same time, I could discreetly look the other way," he said.

"You could have us walk at the same time?" Why was I so excited? I hated Guildford.

"I could," he said, "if you could keep quiet about it."

I agreed and it was arranged, and so I found myself walking at sunset one day, instead of midafternoon. It had been a dry summer except for that one storm when Mary claimed to have seen her father on the battlements, and some leaves on the trees were yellow already, though it was only mid-August. The flowers had their heads drooping. The day had been hot, and now the sky in the west was tinged with pink and purple. Across some hedges I saw Guildford walking toward me. We would soon meet. What would I say?

His solitary footsteps on the brick garden walk echoed in my head as he came closer. I sneaked a look at him. He seemed sad and older and thinner. His hair was too long. It needed cutting. And his coat seemed to need a good dusting.

"Jane," he said in a loud whisper.

I was aware of Master Partridge, standing a good distance away. He was watching us, but when I turned to look, he knelt down to fix his shoe buckle. It must have been really broken, that shoe buckle, because it took a long time to fix.

"Guildford." I went over to the hedge and we looked at each other over the top of it. "How are you faring, Guildford?"

He shrugged. "I hate this place."

"Your father is here now."

"I hate my father. He's the cause of everything. Did Gardiner come and visit you?"

"Yes. He took everything of value."

"Me too. I have nothing left. If we ever get out of here, I won't be worth a shilling, Jane. How will we live?"

"Worry about getting out of here," I found myself whispering. "The rest will take care of itself."

"You are always so hopeful."

"I? No. Never enough. But I do hope to get out soon. Mary will pardon us."

"My father will be beheaded on the twenty-third of this month. Beheaded, Jane. I fear we both will share the same fate."

"No, Guildford. Don't."

He gave a small smile. "I have carved your name on the

wall of my room, Jane. People will see it. It will be there always, for generations."

What could I say? "As long as you keep busy," I answered. "Master Partridge is a good man to let us meet like this. But we must say good-bye now so we don't get him in trouble."

"Jane?" His voice cracked, and he reached for my hand over the hedge.

He looked so young of a sudden. So much like a child. He was genuinely frightened. I gave him my hand briefly. "Have a care, Guildford," I said.

Tears filled his eyes and near spilled over. "I have not been a good husband to you. Do you forgive me?"

"There is nothing to forgive," I said.

"Do you think we could pass notes, with the help of Master Partridge?"

"I wouldn't want to get him into trouble."

"Jane." He tried to speak again, but couldn't. His voice broke.

"I must go, Guildford. We have no more time. God keep you." And I turned and ran away from him, down another path.

August went on and routine took over. The days were hot but already the evenings and mornings were cooler and the slant of the sun looked different, a little less bold and more mellow.

Mrs. Partridge gave me a warm blanket for the nights.

That's when my demons came, haunting me. Outside on Tower Hill was the execution block, where Northumberland would soon go. Where Sir Thomas had gone. And his brother Edward.

Sir Thomas! That was so long ago! Like another lifetime!

Nights, I knew I would end up on that execution block too. What would keep me from it? They'd behead Northumberland and that would make Mary think of his son Guildford, and then her mind would settle on me.

An owl called from somewhere on the grounds outside, where there were looming shapes and dark shadows. And the sound echoed in my soul and found places of sadness and depths of fear I did not know existed.

At supper on September third Master Partridge told us that the Queen had given Edward Courtney back his earldom. "And expensive clothes and land and a diamond ring and sixteen thousand crowns," he added.

Lucky Edward.

"Some say she is to wed him," he said, "Others say Philip the Second of Spain. My money is on Philip, as is every bloke's in every public tavern."

I was sixteen in October, but I did not feel like sixteen. Sometimes I still felt like the child who had gone to live with Queen Katharine and King Henry, who had romped in the gardens with Elizabeth at Chelsea Manor.

November came and there were still fall roses in the Tower gardens. The sun still felt warm in the middle of the day.

November came and the wives of Guildford's brothers, John, Robert, Ambrose, and Henry, were allowed to visit and stay with their husbands in Beauchamp Tower. November came and with it word that Guildford and I were to proceed to the Guildhall for our trial.

They sent us by barge down the river. Mrs. Ellen went with us. I wore the new black gown she had sewn for me. It had an overskirt of black velvet. My hood was of black satin, trimmed with pearls.

At least four hundred halberdiers guarded the streets after we left the barge and walked to the Guildhall. The people had come out by the thousands to see us. I did not know we would cause such a commotion and it was passing strange to see so many faces after being isolated for so long.

The halberdiers had to hold the people back as they pressed toward us, and I heard whispers from some women: "Look, she's just a little girl! A child!"

Well, I suppose I was a child, so now I wanted to cry.

The hall was large and drafty and frightening. The trial was brief and deadly. We pled guilty to treason. Judge Morgan then read the dreadful sentence.

We were sentenced to death.

In front of the judge's bar there was an axe. When we came in, the edge was turned away from us; but after the judge passed sentence, the executioner, who stood by, turned the edge toward us in a symbolic gesture.

We knew what it meant.

The executioner followed us to the water gate when we went back to the barge, and the crowd assembled around him.

There were cries of: "Well, what is it? Death or mercy?"

"Arraigned and condemned," he said loudly. "Judgment to die."

I knew it was a formality. I knew it had to be carried out thus. But the words chilled me to the bone.

"Jane cannot die," I heard a woman from the crowd wail. "She is but a child. Do we execute children now?"

There was no answer.

Back in my lodgings there was considerable weeping and wailing from Mrs. Ellen. "I am innocent," I told her. "Queen Mary knows the crown was thrust upon me. She will not let me die. She will pardon me, you will see. Maybe even at the last minute. Come, let's go downstairs for supper."

We heard that the citizens in London were against Queen Mary's Spanish marriage, that they were calling Philip II

"Jack Spaniard." We heard that the council was begging her to wed Courtney, the Englishman.

One day Sir John Bridges, the Lieutenant of the Tower, came to our lodging and told me that my father had requested permission to visit, if I would see him.

I was half afraid to say yes. There were whispers from Master Partridge and his wife of rebellions being formed to keep Mary from marrying her Spanish prince. And I knew if rebellions were being formed, my father would be part of them.

But how could I say no to my father? I said yes, and when he came, I asked to be left alone with him, which I was.

"Jane." He put his hands on the sides of my face and held them there for a moment. It was the only tenderness I ever remember from him. Ever.

He looked older than his forty-five years now. His hair was almost all gray and his hands trembled.

I inquired after my mother and sisters. "Mary and Catherine are ladies-in-waiting for Queen Mary," he said. "It is a good sign, Jane, that she will forgive you."

"I hope so," I said.

"Jane, listen to me." And he took my hand and sat me down beside him. "The people are not happy with Mary's choice for a husband. Some are going to try to stop her from marrying Philip. Do you know what will happen to this country with a Spanish prince?"

"I have been told," I said.

"The Spanish will come into this realm with armor and guns and will make us Englishmen worse than enemies, for this realm will be brought into such bondage as never before."

There was no arguing. He was passionate.

"Jane," he whispered, "the city fathers are anxious. In country shires, the people are polishing up weapons and looking for leaders. Peter Carew in the west and Sir Thomas Wyatt in Kent are organizing rebellions on a large scale. I am going to join Sir Thomas. We may have you back on the throne yet."

"No!" I said vehemently.

"Jane"—and he took both my hands in his—"you must be ready if it comes to that. We cannot have Spanish rule."

"I am condemned to death already. But there is still a chance of mercy from Queen Mary. She is my cousin. She will not kill me. I have written to her and declared my loyalty."

"Declare all the loyalty you want. Wyatt has a faultless plan. They are issuing an anti-Spanish proclamation in Leicester and Coventry on the twenty-sixth. Jane, I ask nothing of you. Just to keep your mouth shut and your eyes and ears open. And to be there if we need you. You can see I am booted and spurred and ready to ride."

"I will always care for you, Father," I said.

It had to be said or he would never cease his prattle about rebellion. And I wanted no more of it. When he bade me good-bye, I told him to mind himself.

"We don't want you in the Tower," I said.

TWENTY-FOUR

Christmas came and went. It would have been my first Christmas as Queen. I could imagine the merriment at court, the feasts, the masques, the entertainments. Did Mary worry for her kingdom?

She sent out eight thousand men to put down the revolts. They stayed out until the end of January, putting down the rebellious troops.

There was a proclamation out there somewhere, naming me as the Queen's rival. Oh, I had hoped my father wouldn't do it. I had prayed he wouldn't do it. Would I never stop being a pawn for ambitious men?

I tried not to think of it. But each night at supper, I couldn't wait until Master Partridge told us the news.

One moment there was hope for the rebellions, the

next, news of defeat. Men deserted their respective armies, turned their coats, and went begging the Queen for mercy when they saw the rebellions were failing.

And then, on February sixth, Master Partridge gave us the news. Wyatt was captured. My father had been caught hiding under a bundle of hay near a church, where he had stayed, shivering, for two days and nights before he was sniffed out by a dog.

A traitorous, scheming man named Huntingdon had defected from the rebellious forces and gone to fight for the Queen. He had delivered my father up to the Lieutenant of the Tower only a few hours before Wyatt was brought in at Traitors Gate. Then Huntingdon went to Westminster for a meeting with the Queen.

She thanked him and gave him a diamond ring.

It was over.

And of course, the blame for it all was put on me. Certain members of the council wrote to Prince Philip that "Jane of Suffolk and her husband are to lose their heads."

I did not believe it. I had sat in my lodgings for the past months, sewing, reading, studying, and praying. I had not recruited men to fight for me. I had not plotted. I wished Mary well. Could I help what others had done?

No. Mary had always been straight thinking and honest and caring toward me. She had once said we were like sisters. I would not believe she would now be anything less.

The council members could write all the letters they wanted to Prince Philip of Spain. Queen Mary could, and likely would, sign our death warrants. There was always mercy and pardon at the end. She would grant me a reprieve. I was sure of it.

My father and his brothers were brought to the Tower on the sixth of February. On that same day Queen Mary signed death warrants for me and for Guildford.

Formality, I told everyone. Just formality. And to prove it, I had to go about acting as if I were going to die. I wrote notes to both my sisters. I read the mail my father sent me. I wrote to Guildford. They said he was crying in his lodgings.

I reminded him how Queen Mary was my cousin and as such would pardon us at the last moment. I told him to be brave.

Then I had to decide on a dress to wear to my execution.

"How can you, child?" Mrs. Ellen asked.

"I can and I will," I told her. "Fix the black I wore to my trial. Put a white ruff about the neck for hope. Let a bit of red show through the slashed sleeves."

She set about doing so. I sent for a Protestant minister, but was denied him. Instead Queen Mary sent her own minister. Her very own! His name was Father Feckenham.

Of course, he was Catholic, but he was so nice that I took to him immediately and we became fast friends.

He assured me that Mary had no intention of carrying out my sentence, that it was all for show. Londoners loved a show, he reminded me. And when they saw me out there, child that I still was, standing at the block, they might well rush the executioner to stop the whole thing. Mary could not have such a riot. She knew better.

She would wait until the last moment, he told me, and then send a reprieve.

Still, Guildford and I were to die in two days. There wasn't much time. I heard that Guildford was still sobbing himself near to death in his rooms and sent him another message.

My rooms looked out directly on the scaffold, and I spent many an hour gazing at it, imagining how I would be led to it, how I would kneel and the crowds would hush and then at the last minute, the very last minute, would come the reprieve. And the crowds would cheer and I would bow and smile, and tears would come down my face and I would say, "Long live Queen Mary."

The day appointed was quiet under the familiar mists of early-morning England. As I looked out my window I could see the outline of forms all around the execution block. People were gathering for the show.

Guildford was to go first. As he passed under my window he turned, looked up, and waved. He was no longer crying.

He was not to be executed on that block, but outside the Tower, because he was not of royal blood. Would Queen Mary carry through with his death? I pushed the feelings from me.

What would happen to Guildford and me when we were pardoned? Would we go home? Where was home? Did I have to be his wife now or could the whole marriage be considered the sham it was?

Then I heard the sound of a cart and looked down.

What had happened? There was a body in the cart. Guildford! A headless body! Oh, I felt so weak, so despairing. They had executed Guildford! He was dead! He who had passed by this very window but a scant while ago and waved to me.

Gone forever. Oh, Guildford! What a waste. I sank down on my knees by the window, and Mrs. Ellen came running over. "What is it, child?"

"Guildford is dead."

She opened her mouth to say something, and then Father Feckenham came into the room. "Jane, it is time," he said.

I froze. I could not do this thing now. Not even though I knew I would be pardoned. It would seem such a mockery in the face of Guildford's death.

But then, before I knew what was happening, Father

Feckenham was taking me by the hand and telling me to be brave. He had it on good account that I was going to be pardoned. "Come now," he said quietly, "don't let the crowd see you crying. They'll think you have little faith in our Queen."

He was right. I allowed him to take my hand and lead me out into the mists of morning. Oh, there were so many people! I couldn't see their faces, but I could hear them crying, "Jane, Jane, Jane."

We walked to the execution block, and behind me I heard Mrs. Ellen sniffling and I urged her to be quiet. "When the sun breaks through the mist, I will walk from this place," I told them.

Drums were beating, low and steadily in the distance. I thought they were the sound of my blood beating in my head.

The executioner nodded a greeting to me then and asked my forgiveness. I forgave him, as was the custom. Then the drums stopped and all was silent. I heard a crow caw.

"Kneel, Jane," Father Feckenham said to me. "You must make it look real."

"Where is the courier with the pardon?"

"You know how Queen Mary likes drama," he said. "He will be here on time. Don't fear, Jane."

Sometimes we have to believe, I reminded myself, even when we know better.

I knelt and they put a blindfold around my eyes. But then I couldn't find the block. In what seemed like an endless amount of time I felt around in the straw for it. "Where is it?" I asked. "Where is the block? I can't find it. Help me, please."

Someone grasped each of my wrists and put them to either side of me and then guided my head to the block. I knelt, waiting. The whole world waited.

Soon now, soon, he would come, the courier. Running up the hill, mayhap even as the executioner had his axe raised. The crowd would cheer. They would raise me up and take the blindfold from me. The sun would be out, and I would be allowed to go home.

I waited. If only I could see! In another moment I would ask Father Feckenham where the courier was with the reprieve. But for now I would be good. I would make them all proud of me.

And then, and then, and then. Ohhh.

LADY JANE GREY

1537–1554

AUTHOR'S NOTE

Lady Jane was beheaded that day by the executioner. There never was a reprieve. Ten days later the same fate was accorded her father, Henry Grey.

Two weeks after Henry Grey's death, Jane's mother, Lady Frances, married his groom of chambers, and during Queen Mary's reign, she was always at court, with no evidence of bad feelings between her and the Queen for having executed her daughter, husband, and son-in-law.

Queen Mary became known as "Bloody Mary" because of the violence and deaths that occurred during her reign. She did marry Philip of Spain and restored the Catholics to England, then burned hundreds of Protestants. She reigned for five years and had no children. When she died, the Protestant Princess Elizabeth took over the throne of England and reigned successfully for forty-five years.

Everything in the book that follows the historical line of events is true, even down to Princess Elizabeth and Sir Thomas carrying on in her bedroom when she was just fourteen or fifteen.

I have fictionalized some events for the sake of story, and interpreted others to tighten my plot, but otherwise, no amount of invention or creativity could add to this incredible story.

Robert Dudley, brother of Guildford, was pardoned by Queen Mary and released from the Tower. He went on to become Earl of Leicester and a favorite of Queen Elizabeth, whom he served faithfully all his life. But that is another story.

⁓BIBLIOGRAPHY⁓

Chapman, Hester W. *Lady Jane Grey.* Boston: Little, Brown and Company, 1962.

George, Margaret. *The Autobiography of Henry VIII.* New York: Ballantine Books, 1986.

Irwin, Margaret. *Young Bess.* London: Allison and Busby Ltd., 1998.

Maxwell, Robin. *The Secret Diary of Anne Boleyn.* New York: Scribner Paperback Fiction, 1997.

Malvern, Gladys. *The World of Lady Jane Grey.* New York: The Vanguard Press, 1964.

Weir, Alison. *The Six Wives of Henry VIII.* New York: Ballantine Books, 1991.

———. *The Children of Henry VIII.* New York: Ballantine Books, 1986.

———. *Henry VIII: The King and His Court.* New York: Ballantine Books, 2001.

R eaders have come to know Ann Rinaldi for her richly satisfying historical fiction. Eight of her novels have been named ALA Best Books for Young Adults, including *Time Enough for Drums*, *The Last Silk Dress*, *Break with Charity*, and *Wolf by the Ears*. The author of more than thirty books for young readers, including a book in the Dear America series, she was awarded the National History Award from the Daughters of the American Revolution. She lives in Somerville, New Jersey, where she is currently working on a book about Queen Elizabeth.